**'You didn't sa...
your cousin.'**

'You didn't ask,' she retorted, probably unreasonably because there was no reason on earth why he should have asked. Before she could stop herself she added, 'In fact, you haven't asked anything.'

Dave was silent for a moment, then he said, 'We haven't got off to a very good start, have we?'

'You could say that again,' said Siobhan tightly.

Laura MacDonald lives in the Isle of Wight. She is married and has a grown-up family. She has enjoyed writing fiction since she was a child, but for several years she worked for members of the medical profession, both in pharmacy and in general practice. Her daughter is a nurse and has helped with the research for Laura's medical stories.

Recent titles by the same author:

FROM THIS DAY FORWARD
TO HAVE AND TO HOLD
WINNING THROUGH
POWERS OF PERSUASION
DRASTIC MEASURES

FORSAKING ALL OTHERS

BY
LAURA MACDONALD

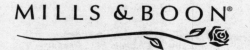

MILLS & BOON®

First published in Great Britain 1998
Harlequin Mills & Boon Limited,
Eton House, 18-24 Paradise Road, Richmond, Surrey TW9 1SR

© Laura MacDonald 1998

ISBN 0 263 81032 1

Set in Times Roman 10½ on 12 pt.
03-9807-49389-D

Printed and bound in Great Britain
by Mackays of Chatham PLC, Chatham

CHAPTER ONE

'I'M SO sorry about Uncle Harry.' Siobhan turned to Helen, her expression anxious. 'You say he's in full-time care now?'

Helen nodded. 'Yes, unfortunately, it had to come to that. I desperately wanted to keep Dad here at home with me, but the effects of Alzheimer's are pretty devastating, you know, and in the end it just became impossible—what with my job and everything.'

'I can imagine,' Siobhan replied. 'Mum was very upset. Uncle Harry is a great favourite of hers. She's been talking about coming over from Ireland for a visit.'

'That would be nice,' said Helen. 'Your mother and I haven't seen each other for years.' She looked up as the door opened suddenly and a large red setter nosed its way into the sitting room.

'Oh,' cried Siobhan, 'it's Chester! Hello, old boy. You remember me, don't you?' She reached out to pat the dog's head.

'Poor old Chester,' Helen sighed. 'He can't understand where Dad has gone to—I'm afraid he doesn't get anywhere near as much exercise as when Dad was here.'

'It's very good of you to let me stay in the stable flat,' Siobhan said a moment later as she leaned back in the floral patterned armchair and crossed her legs. 'Mum thought you would have been sure to let it to visitors throughout the season.'

'Normally I do.' Helen picked up the teapot from a low table and began to pour the tea. 'But this year, because of Dad's condition, I didn't advertise it. There was no way he could have coped with lots of children running around.'

'So it's been empty, then?' Siobhan flicked back tendrils of her long chestnut hair that had escaped from its black ribbon.

'Actually, no.' Helen paused in her tea-pouring. 'In the end,' she continued, 'I let it to a locum GP who's been working for the local group practice. He was very quiet and so unobtrusive Dad hardly knew he was there.'

'So, has he moved on now—this locum?' asked Siobhan when Helen didn't offer any further information.

'Er…not exactly.' Helen glanced at Siobhan from under her eyebrows. 'It's rather romantic, really. He's fallen in love with one of the partners at the practice, Kate Chapman—she's a friend of mine actually. Anyway, he's moved in with her and they are already planning their wedding.'

'I suppose you didn't have anything to do with that, by any chance?'

'Me?' Helen looked up in mock surprise. 'Whatever do you mean?'

'Well, Mum used to say you were a born matchmaker,' said Siobhan with a laugh.

'Did she now?' Helen pulled a face. 'I can see I shall have to have words with your mother. I can't have her making allegations like that, even if she is my cousin.'

They both laughed and Helen passed Siobhan her tea. 'I must say, though,' she said after a moment, 'it really is nice to have you here. Dad was so proud, you know, when he heard you were taking paramedic training, and when he knew you had got a job here on the Island he was overjoyed. At least he knew all that before…before his memory went completely.'

'It's like a dream come true, really,' said Siobhan with a little sigh. 'I always wanted to come here, you know, ever since those holidays when I was a child, and probably also because it's Mum's birthplace. And it's also nice to have a change…to meet new people…'

'I should imagine you'll find the Isle of Wight very similar to Ireland,' said Helen a moment later. 'It has the same timeless feel about it.'

Siobhan grinned as she sipped her tea. 'You mean like it's twenty years behind everywhere else?'

'Oh, at least.' Helen laughed, then, growing serious, added, 'But with the season getting into full swing you'll find the place more lively—in fact, with the job you'll be doing, downright hectic. I know Accident and Emergency gets that way during the summer so it follows that it's the same for the paramedics.'

'You're sister-in-charge now on A and E, aren't you?' Admiration shone in Siobhan's grey eyes as she looked at Helen.

'For my sins—yes.' Helen pulled a face, then said, 'But, getting back to you, have you met your new colleagues yet?'

'Some of them,' Siobhan replied. 'I reported to my chief this morning and I met some of the crews. They seem a very friendly bunch. There are two other women, apparently, one who is a paramedic and another who is a driver-attendant, although I didn't meet either of them today. Also the guy who is to be my partner wasn't on duty either so I've yet to meet him.'

'Did they say what his name is?' asked Helen. 'I probably know him—I know most of the crews.'

Siobhan nodded and replaced her cup in its saucer.

'Yes,' she said. 'It was Dave something or other… Now, what did they say?' She glanced at Helen enquiringly, but realised that her cousin had grown very still and was staring at her.

'It wasn't Dave Morey, was it?' she said slowly after a moment.

'Um…yes, I think it was.' Siobhan nodded. 'Yes, that was it. Dave Morey. Do you know him?' she added curiously when Helen's expression remained frozen.

'Oh, yes,' Helen replied. 'I know him. Everyone knows Dave Morey.'

'That sounds very ominous.' Siobhan gave a laugh. 'What's wrong with him, for heaven's sake?'

'Oh, nothing,' said Helen hastily. 'There's nothing wrong with him at all, really. He's a very nice guy. Very popular…'

'So why did you look like that when you knew he was to be my partner?'

'Like what?' Helen was obviously trying to appear casual now.

'Like you wished my partner could be anyone other than this Dave…Dave…'

'Morey.' Helen completed the sentence for Siobhan.

'Yes… Dave Morey.'

'Well…' Helen hesitated, as if struggling to find the right words to explain her reaction. 'Let's just say,' she went on at last, 'that he wouldn't have been my choice for you. I had hoped it would be one of the older men…'

'You mean someone more experienced?' Siobhan raised her eyebrows.

'Oh.' Helen's mouth tightened. 'Dave Morey's experienced all right…' She trailed off helplessly.

'So, how old is he?' asked Siobhan, her curiosity aroused.

'Let's see now,' Helen paused, considering. 'I suppose he must be late twenties.'

'Married?'

'No.' Her reply was swift, almost too swift, and when Siobhan's eyebrows lifted again, she added, 'No, Dave most certainly isn't married.'

'Is he good at his job?'

'As far as I know, yes. He and Pete were quite a team...everyone knew them.'

'Who's Pete?' asked Siobhan quickly.

'Pete Steel,' said Helen. 'He and Dave Morey have worked together for years. Pete was recently diagnosed with multiple sclerosis. He's had to give up his job. It's tragic, really—he's married with a young family.'

'Now you come to mention it, the chief said something about someone with multiple sclerosis, but I hadn't realised it was the person whose place I'm taking.' Siobhan paused, then throwing Helen a quick look, she said, 'But you still haven't told me what's wrong with Dave Morey.'

Helen sighed. 'There's nothing really wrong with Dave,' she said. 'In fact, I would go so far as to say he has a heart of gold, really, even if he is what my mother would have called a bit of a rough diamond. It's just that...'

'Yes?' persisted Siobhan.

'He's been a bit of a bad boy in his time...'

'In what way?'

'Well, he's got a bit of a reputation.'

'For what?'

'With the girls.'

'Ah,' said Siobhan, 'now we're getting to it.'

'He's a charmer,' said Helen defensively, 'and a bit of a lad.'

'Handsome?' Siobhan raised her eyebrows.

'No, not really…although…' Helen hesitated, then grudgingly admitted, 'I suppose he's what you might call attractive—in an unusual sort of way.'

'I can't wait to meet him,' said Siobhan with a grin.

'He does have this reputation for loving girls then leaving them,' said Helen briskly. 'I can tell you, Siobhan,' she added, 'over the years I've had more than one young nurse crying on my shoulder because of Dave Morey.'

'And you're worried I may succumb to his charm—is that it?' asked Siobhan coolly.

'Let's just say I wouldn't like to see that happen…because you certainly wouldn't be the first.' Helen stood up, adding, 'I thought a little timely warning wouldn't come amiss.'

'Well, thanks.' Siobhan laughed and also rose to her feet. 'I must say, you've made me intrigued to meet this man. But you needn't worry,' she added quickly when she saw the look of alarm that came into Helen's eyes again, 'because I've come here to work. But, quite apart from that, I can assure you, Helen, I'm well able to take care of myself.'

'I'm glad to hear it,' said Helen drily, adding with a grin, 'Now, if you've finished your tea I'll take you across to the stable flat and you can get unpacked and settled in.'

Two days later Siobhan drove her rather elderly Mini through the gates of the ambulance station and parked in the staff car park. She was looking forward to starting her new job but, at the same time, was willing to confess to a certain amount of apprehension.

A quick glance in her driving mirror reassured her that

her appearance was appropriate to the occasion, with her usually unruly mass of auburn hair tamed into a single, thick plait and her pale complexion enhanced with just the right amount of make-up—a hint of blusher and a touch of mascara to the already thick fringe of lashes around her smoky-grey eyes.

It was a clear June morning, with the sun already hinting at the warmth to come. Siobhan had enjoyed the drive from Helen's home in the village of Gatcombe, through country lanes between hedgerows bright with new growth, to Shalbrooke, with the general hospital and the ambulance station situated close by.

She'd already settled into Helen's flat which formed part of the stable block of the old Coach House. The flat was lovely and was more than adequate for her use until she could find more permanent accommodation of her own. Helen had been quite right when she'd said that Siobhan would find the Isle of Wight very similar to her native Ireland, with its rural landscape, sandy beaches and small towns and villages. It felt comfortingly familiar, and all she needed to do now was to meet her colleagues and get started on her new job.

With one final glance in the mirror, she opened the car door and slipped out of the driving seat. She locked the door behind her, lifted her bag containing her new uniform out of the boot of the Mini and made her way across the car park to the main entrance of the station.

The first person she saw as she entered the building was a young woman, her short, dark hair shaped in an attractive urchin cut that framed her tiny features. She had been reading something on a large, rather untidy notice board and was about to move away when she saw Siobhan.

'Hello,' she said. 'Can I help?'

'I'm Siobhan O'Mara—paramedic. It's my first day.'

'Oh, right.' Briefly the girl's eyes flickered over her. 'I'm Zoe Grainger. Welcome aboard. It's high time we had a few more females around here, I can tell you,' she added. 'You can help Lisa and me keep the men in their place. Now, I expect you want to change into your uniform, don't you?'

'Yes, please.' Siobhan nodded.

'Come with me and I'll take you through to the locker room—it's communal, I'm afraid.' Zoe pulled a face. 'Hopefully, we'll be getting our own soon. I usually change in the loo or at home.' As Siobhan began to follow her down a narrow passage she added curiously, 'Where are you from?'

'Ireland,' Siobhan replied.

'Really?' Zoe looked faintly surprised.

'My father is Irish, but my mother was born and bred here on the Isle of Wight.'

'That explains why your accent isn't that strong.'

'I've spent the best part of my life in Ireland,' said Siobhan, 'although my early years were spent in this country. My father took us back to Ireland when my grandfather died and he took over the family haulage business.'

'So you're used to big vehicles, then?' said Zoe with a laugh.

Siobhan nodded. 'Yes, ambulances seem quite small after some of our lorries.'

'Well, here's the inner sanctum.' Zoe threw open the door of the locker room, then stood back to allow Siobhan to enter. The room was stark, grey and depressing with its row of steel lockers and lines of pegs and hard wooden benches.

'And over there...' Zoe pointed across the passage

'...is the crew room. Get yourself changed then come over and join the rest of the gang.'

'OK. Thanks.' Siobhan nodded and after Zoe had retreated, shutting the door behind her with a bang, she stood for a moment and looked around.

She wondered where she should change then, recalling Zoe's words, made her way to the far end of the room to a row of cubicles which quite obviously were the loos. It was cramped and restricted in the cubicle, but somehow Siobhan managed to change out of the short skirt and skinny top she was wearing into the trousers, shirt and green jacket which was the regulation summer uniform for the paramedics.

She was well used to conditions and procedures, having spent two years in the ambulance service in Ireland, before coming to England to commence her paramedic training.

When she was ready she stowed her belongings into an empty locker and pocketed the key, before making her way out of the locker room and across the passage to the crew room.

There were four men in the room—two who stood chatting on the far side with mugs of coffee in their hands, and two others who were playing pool. They all glanced up as Siobhan came into the room, and one of the two at the pool table recognised her from her previous visit.

'Hello, there,' he called. Turning to the other men, he said, 'This is Dave's new oppo—sorry, love, I can't remember your name.'

'It's Siobhan—Siobhan O'Mara,' she replied.

'How do you spell that?' called one of the men on the far side of the room.

Siobhan smiled and spelt the word for him. She was well used to confusion over her name.

'Crikey,' said the man, 'I always thought it was spelt C-h-e-v-a-u-g-h-a-n—you know, like in Frankie Vaughan.'

'So do most people,' said Siobhan.

'You're Irish?' said the first man.

'Half-Irish.' Siobhan began to explain again, then trailed off as the second man at the pool table straightened up and gave her a curious glance. He looked at the other men and said, 'Is Dave back from leave yet?'

The two men drinking coffee looked at each other, and one of them said, 'He's due back this morning.'

'Oh, boy!' The man at the pool table lifted his cue and, leaning across the table, smartly potted the black.

Before Siobhan had a chance to even speculate on this interchange Zoe suddenly came into the room.

'There you are,' she said. 'The chief wants to see you in his office—come on, I'll show you the way.'

Siobhan followed Zoe back up the passage to the reception area where she knocked on a door. Another woman, presumably a secretary, came out of the room and had a whispered word with Zoe, peering at Siobhan over half-moon glasses attached to a bright blue cord around her neck, then went back into the room and shut the door.

'Apparently, the chief's on the phone,' Zoe explained. 'He won't be long. Why don't you sit down and wait?' She indicated a chair. 'I have to get back—I'm on duty now.'

'All right. Thanks, Zoe.' Siobhan smiled and sat down.

Her chair was facing the main entrance of the station and as she waited several people came and went. One or two merely glanced in her direction, some smiled or nodded and others ignored her.

She was just beginning to wonder how much longer 'the chief' was going to keep her waiting when the large double entrance doors were thrown open yet again and a man strode into Reception. He was obviously in a hurry and barely threw as much as a glance in Siobhan's direction. Then he appeared to do a double take, stopped and came back.

'He-llo,' he said, his eyes travelling over her slight form.

'Hello.' She smiled up at him, aware of admiration and intrigue in his gaze.

'Is someone taking care of you?' His gaze moved to her face, her hair, her eyes, finally coming to rest on her mouth. Such obviousness from a man usually left Siobhan cold, but there was such amusement and appreciation lurking in this one's green eyes that she found it impossible to take offence.

'Yes,' she replied—coolly she hoped. 'Thank you. I'm just waiting to see...to see the chief,' she added, noting the slightly puzzled frown that creased his forehead.

'I haven't seen you here before,' he went on, obviously intent on prolonging the moment in any way he could. 'But then, I have been away—a fortnight's leave,' he explained.

'Anywhere nice?' She found herself allowing her own gaze to wander now over him, realising she liked what she saw—those rather fascinating green eyes, the dark hair cut very short and gelled, the straight brows, the faintest suggestion of shadow on the firm, squarish jaw and the full, sensual curve of his lower lip. He was dressed in casual gear—denims and a sweatshirt—so there was no telling his status, but already the first stir-rings of suspicion were forming in Siobhan's mind.

'Tenerife,' he said.

'Very nice.' She nodded.

'It was.' He sighed. 'It won't be easy this morning, getting back into the swing of things, I can tell you.'

'I can imagine.' She paused. 'Er, I take it you work here?' She allowed her gaze to meet his again and found it almost impossible to look away.

'Afraid so. The name's Morey,' he said. 'Dave Morey.'

She'd known it was him. Guessed, really, from the moment she'd set eyes on him. She held out her hand as he introduced himself, and as he took it and leaned forward slightly she said, 'Siobhan O'Mara. I'm new here. I've only just arrived. It's my first day.'

'You're one of the new paramedics?' His eyes wid-ened with delighted surprise.

'You mean there are others—apart from me?'

'Only one, as far as I know. Yourself and someone by the name of Greg Freeman who is going to be my new oppo.' He paused, his gaze again flickering over her. 'I would think old Barry is in for a surprise.'

'Barry?' she asked.

'Barry Weston—he'll be your oppo. He's all right, old Barry,' he added quickly. 'Bit of a hypochondriac, but OK underneath.'

'Oh,' said Siobhan drawing in her breath. 'I under-stood that—'

But that was as far as she got for at that moment the door opened again and the rather officious-looking sec-retary appeared once more.

'Ms O'Mara?' she said, and when Siobhan stood up she turned and peered over the top of her spectacles at

Dave. 'So you're back, then?' she said, her tone carefully impartial. 'The chief was looking for you earlier.'

'Oh, really?' Dave remained apparently unperturbed.

'You'll have to come back later,' the secretary said crisply. 'He's seeing Ms O'Mara next.'

'OK.' Dave Morey nodded. 'I'll go and change.' He turned to go, glanced back at Siobhan and winked. 'I'll see *you* later,' he said with a grin. Then he was gone down the passage towards the locker room, whistling the latest chart-topper.

Siobhan watched him and then turned to the secretary—in time to see her roll her eyes heavenwards, before opening the door and standing back for Siobhan to precede her into the chief's office.

Ted Carter was seated behind his desk. He rose as Siobhan came into the room and held out his hand.

'Siobhan—hello again,' he said. 'Nice to have you aboard. Come and sit down for a moment.' He indicated a chair.

Obediently she sat down, thinking as she did so how nice Ted Carter was. There was something about him that reminded her of her father and just for a moment she felt a deep pang of homesickness.

'You wanted to see me?' she asked.

'Yes. But only to make sure everything is all right before you enter the fray.' He smiled.

'Oh, yes. Yes, I think so,' she said, then added, 'In fact I really can't wait to get started.'

'Monica needs to check a few details with you. Nothing alarming—only information concerning tax and pensions, that sort of thing.' He paused. 'Uniform OK?' he went on, and when she nodded he said, 'You also have to be issued with your medical case and your equipment and drugs, which we shall need you to sign for.'

'Yes, of course.' Siobhan nodded.

'Well, I think that's all… You're now an official crew member of this division. Do you have any queries, any problems?'

'No, I don't think so.' Siobhan hesitated. 'Only…'

'Yes?' Ted had sat down again but he looked up, as if detecting the hesitation in her voice.

'Oh, it's nothing, really…just that when I came in a couple of days ago you said I would be working with someone called Dave Morey.'

'Yes.' Ted Carter nodded but Siobhan noticed that a guarded, wary look had entered his eyes. 'Yes,' he went on, 'that's correct. Do you have a problem with that?'

'Oh, no.' Siobhan shook her head. 'Not really. It's only that I met Dave Morey just now…outside in the corridor…and he seemed to be under the impression that his new partner was someone by the name of Greg Freeman—'

'Dave Morey has been away on leave,' Ted interrupted briskly, 'and before he went, yes, that was the plan, but changes have been made since then.'

'I see…' Siobhan began. She wasn't certain she did see but felt she had to say something. At the same time, she had the uneasy feeling she had far from heard the last over this issue of who was to work with whom.

'It's nothing for you to worry about.'

'No…'

'You don't sound too sure.' Ted Carter gave her a keen look.

'It's just that Dave Morey seemed…'

'Seemed what?' Ted raised one eyebrow.

'I don't know. I'm not sure…' Siobhan shrugged.

'Like I said, there's nothing for you to worry about,' said Ted Carter, then added, 'You leave Dave Morey to me.'

Before either of them had the chance to say anything further there came the sound of angry, raised voices from outside the door. Ted Carter rose to his feet, strode round the desk and pulled open the door.

Siobhan turned in her chair and through the open doorway she could see Monica, the secretary. She appeared to be arguing with someone who was just out of Siobhan's line of vision.

'It's all right, Monica,' said Ted firmly. 'I'll see him now.' He turned back to Siobhan. 'That'll be all for now—get yourself along to the depot and see the training officer, who will issue your supplies.'

Siobhan jumped to her feet and in her haste to leave the room almost collided with Dave Morey on his way in. She'd only seen him moments before and he had been smiling, pleased to meet her, charming to the last degree. Now the change couldn't have been in greater contrast. He was grim-faced and unsmiling and where before she could have sworn that amusement lurked in those fascinating green eyes, now, as he strode into the chief's office, they glittered with barely controlled anger.

'Come in, Dave,' said Ted Carter. 'We'll get this sorted right now.'

'Too right we will.' Dave Morey's voice was tight, cold.

Not waiting to hear more, Siobhan fled.

CHAPTER TWO

SIOBHAN threw a tentative glance at the man beside her at the wheel of the ambulance. This was their first call and Dave Morey's tight-lipped expression, which he'd worn since he'd emerged from Ted Carter's office, did little to alleviate her apprehension.

She had wanted to say something, but wasn't sure what. Part of her wanted to voice her indignation if she was being subjected to any form of sexual discrimination, but another part of her held back, sympathising with the fact that agreed arrangements might have been changed behind Dave Morey's back.

He'd hardly spoken to her while she'd collected her equipment and even later, when he'd taken her to their vehicle, his comments were terse and to the point. As for the admiration that she'd seen in his eyes earlier, she wondered if she'd imagined it.

'Where are we going?' she asked at last, breaking the uncomfortable silence.

'Yarmouth,' he replied. 'To the car ferry,' he added after a moment.

'Didn't the control room say something about someone collapsing?' Siobhan threw him another glance but the dark brows were still low, drawn together in a frown as he concentrated on the road ahead.

He nodded. 'Yes, it's a passenger on a coach—with a party of pensioners apparently. The ferry captain requested an ambulance.'

20

'You must get a lot of calls to holiday-makers,' said Siobhan.

'Well, yes, but that is pretty inevitable, being a holiday island,' he replied shortly.

Siobhan bit her lip and looked out of the window. They were approaching a small town now—apparently Yarmouth from the road signs. The narrow streets were thronged with tourists and the harbour packed with yachts and dinghies. The bright morning sunlight sparkled on the water and the air was filled with the cries of seabirds and the sounds of shipping. The car ferry had docked and was unloading its vehicles as Dave drew the ambulance as close as he could to the ramps and switched off the engine.

'Right,' he said, 'we'll go on and assess first, then, if necessary, we'll take the ambulance on board. Don't forget your case,' he added.

Siobhan stared at him for a moment, wondering if he was serious. When his expression remained the same she decided that he really had thought she might need reminding to take her medical case to a call. What did he think her training had been about, for heaven's sake? And, come to that, how did he think she'd spent the previous two years in Ireland with the ambulance service? She could see she would have to have a quiet word with Dave Morey in the not too distant future and set him straight on a few issues.

But now was not the time. They had a patient waiting for them, a patient who was depending on their skills and expertise to get her to hospital for further treatment.

As they boarded the ferry two coaches were disembarking, their passengers staring with interest at the two paramedics. They were met by the purser, who escorted them into the vessel and upstairs into the restaurant lounge.

'The lady collapsed while queuing to buy a cup of tea,' the purser explained as he led the way down the length of the lounge. 'She's conscious and we managed to make her fairly comfortable on one of the seats, but she's in a lot of pain.'

Dave Morey crouched beside the woman while Siobhan automatically began to set up the oxygen supply. 'Hello, love,' he said. 'What's your name?'

The woman was elderly, large and with a florid complexion. She had her eyes closed, her face was twisted with pain and her hands were tightly clutched to her chest. At the sound of Dave's voice close to her ear she opened her eyes.

'Can you tell us your name?' he repeated, at the same time lifting one of her hands away from her chest and apparently checking her pulse rate.

'It's Ivy...' The woman's voice was little more than a whispered gasp.

Siobhan snapped the catches on her medical case, swung back the lid and took out a sphygmomanometer.

'Do you suffer from angina, Ivy?' As Dave spoke and the patient managed to nod in response, to Siobhan's amazement he leaned across the seat and, taking the sphygmomanometer out of her hands, he proceeded to secure the cuff on the woman's arm in order to check her blood pressure.

Siobhan stared at him, wishing he would make up his mind whether he was driver or attendant. When they'd left the station and he'd automatically climbed into the driving seat of the ambulance she had been happy to let him do so, imagining, in her innocence, that he would drive until she knew the district, or even that he thought she needed the experience as attendant, with him assisting if necessary.

Now it seemed he was reluctant to let her do either. Burning with indignation, she held the oxygen mask over the patient's nose and mouth.

'Do you have medication, Ivy?' asked Dave a moment later after he'd finished checking her blood pressure, which Siobhan, looking over his shoulder, had seen was abnormally high.

The patient nodded again.

'Where is it?' Dave looked round, his gaze coming to rest on a white handbag on the floor beside the seat. 'Try in there,' he said sharply to Siobhan.

Watched by the purser and another female member of the crew, Siobhan opened the bag and rummaged quickly through the contents which included aspirin, indigestion tablets, bunion pads and denture-cleaning tablets—but no angina medication.

'Nothing here,' said Siobhan. Crouching beside the patient, she said urgently, 'Ivy, where are your heart pills?'

Ivy pushed aside the mask. 'In my case,' she gasped.

Siobhan looked quickly at the purser.

'Her luggage will be with all the rest in the boot of one of the coaches—I could send someone to look,' he said.

'It'll take too long,' said Dave.

'We have glyceryl trinitrate,' said Siobhan.

Dave nodded. 'Yes, we'll get a tablet under her tongue—that should do the trick.'

'Don't we have a spray?' Siobhan began to search in her case. 'I always think they seem to act faster... Oh, yes, here's one.' She took the GTN spray out of her case and was about to administer it when once again she found it taken from her grasp and she was forced merely to observe as Dave persuaded Ivy to lift her tongue before he administered the much-needed medication.

Somehow Siobhan managed to bite back the protest that sprang to her lips. Instead, she did her best to try to calm the patient while they waited for the glyceryl trinitrate to take effect.

When at last Ivy seemed to be breathing more easily and experiencing less pain the purser, looking decidedly relieved, glanced at Dave and said, 'Would you like to bring your ambulance on board? I'm sure that would make things easier for you.'

Dave nodded. 'Yes, it would.' He hesitated, glancing first at Ivy and then at Siobhan, as if trying to come to a decision. 'Perhaps you'd like to go and fetch the ambulance,' he said at last. 'Bring a chair back with you,' he added as he passed her the keys. 'I think it would be best if we can manage without a stretcher down those stairs to the car deck.'

Taking a deep breath Siobhan locked her case then, without looking at Dave Morey again, scrambled to her feet and made her way back through the ship's lounge to the stairs.

The car deck was deserted apart from members of the crew, who were waiting to load the vehicles for the return journey to Lymington.

Quickly Siobhan made her way up the ramp to the waiting ambulance where she slipped behind the wheel, started the engine and drove smartly on board the ferry, positioning the rear of the vehicle in line with the doors to the stairway.

After collecting a folding chair and a blue cellular blanket from the back of the ambulance, she made her way back to the restaurant lounge.

By this time Ivy was looking much better and between them Siobhan, Dave and the purser lifted her into the chair, tucked the blanket around her and strapped her securely into place.

'Can't have you falling out on the way downstairs,' joked Dave. Without looking at Siobhan but obviously addressing her and quietly so that Ivy didn't hear, he said, 'You'd better take the head end. There will be a lot of weight to manoeuvre on those stairs.'

There *was* a lot of weight, and it was difficult, but somehow at last they got Ivy into the back of the ambulance.

Siobhan waited, wondering just what Dave would expect. He quite obviously didn't trust her to do anything. It would be interesting now to see which, for him, would be the lesser of two evils—allowing her to attend the patient on the drive back to the hospital or entrusting her to drive his precious vehicle and risk getting lost.

'I think,' he said, hesitating, 'I think you'd better drive back.'

'Are you sure about that?' Siobhan looked at him, her eyes widening innocently.

'Why?' he said sharply. 'What's wrong—you're capable, aren't you?'

'Of course,' she replied. 'In fact, believe it or not, there are a lot of things I'm capable of.'

Without waiting for him to reply, she jumped out of the back of the ambulance, slammed the doors, secured them and hurried round to the driver's seat.

Moments later she reversed the ambulance up the ramp and off the ferry and raised her hand in acknowledgement to a member of the crew, who nodded back and immediately began to beckon the first of the waiting cars on board.

With a tight little smile hovering around the corners of her mouth, she took the road for Shalbrooke.

She enjoyed the drive. It was good to be behind the wheel of an ambulance again—she'd missed that during her short but intensive paramedic training in London. In fact, she'd always loved driving large vehicles. She'd learned to drive in one of her father's lorries on the private tracks of the haulage depot when she had been little more than fourteen years old. That love had probably influenced her choice of career, combining it with her desire to care for people and her love of dramatic situations.

But her first day as a fully fledged paramedic had left much to be desired, she thought grimly as she swung the ambulance into the gates of the Shalbrooke General Hospital, and that was something that would have to be sorted out—and sorted out quickly if she was to continue working with Dave Morey.

She parked in the bay in front of Accident and Emergency and, climbing from the vehicle, hurried round to open the doors, where she was joined by a staff nurse who threw her a quick, curious glance. 'Hi, I'm Georgina Merrick—you must be Siobhan,' she said. 'What have you got for us?'

By this time the doors were open, revealing Dave in the back of the vehicle with Ivy. It was he who answered the staff nurse's question, again not giving Siobhan a chance to answer.

'Angina attack, Georgie,' he said. 'I've given Nitrolingual by aerosol and I've kept up the oxygen as she seemed to still be having difficulty with her breathing.'

'Right,' said the staff nurse briskly, 'let's get her inside.'

Between them they lowered Ivy's chair to the ground on the hydraulic lift then Dave and Siobhan took her inside. In Reception they were met by Helen Turner and a junior doctor.

Helen smiled briefly at Siobhan, listened as Dave again outlined details of Ivy's condition, then she said, 'Take her into Room One, please.'

The doctor and staff nurse escorted them into the treatment room where together they lifted Ivy onto a bed.

'This is as far as we go, love,' said Dave, as he folded the chair and Siobhan picked up the blanket.

Briefly Ivy lifted the mask from her face. 'Thank you,' she said. 'Thank you both for everything.'

'All part of the service, ma'am,' said Dave. He smiled and Siobhan decided it was the first smile she'd seen since early that morning when he'd first caught sight of her in the ambulance station reception.

Leaving Ivy in the capable hands of the doctor and the staff nurse, they made their way outside again, where Helen was waiting for them. She looked smart and efficient in her crisp, starched Sister's uniform, her blonde hair smoothed into a neat pleat.

'So, how's it going, then?' she said to Siobhan. 'First day and all that.'

Before Siobhan could answer Dave stopped and looked from her to Helen. 'Oh, sorry,' he muttered. 'This is my new partner—Siobhan O'Mara.'

Helen gave a short laugh. 'I know,' she said.

Dave frowned. 'You mean, you two know each other?'

'We should do,' said Helen. 'Siobhan is my cousin or, to be strictly correct, I should say my second cousin. Didn't you know?' Coolly she raised her eyebrows.

To Siobhan's satisfaction Dave Morey looked astounded.

'No,' he said, throwing her an embarrassed glance. 'No, I didn't.'

'I thought you knew everything, Dave,' said Helen lightly.

'Obviously not,' he muttered, then added, 'In fact, there seem to have been quite a few things going on lately that I knew nothing about.'

'Ah, that's what you must expect if you go flitting off to foreign places,' Helen replied. As the phone on the desk rang she looked at Siobhan. 'See you later,' she said, then lifted the receiver.

They walked back to the ambulance in silence. Dave automatically climbed into the driver's seat and Siobhan took a deep breath, counted to ten and opened the passenger door.

'You didn't say Helen Turner was your cousin,' he said moodily as he drove out of the hospital grounds.

'You didn't ask,' she retorted, probably unreasonably because there was no reason on earth why he should have asked. Before she could stop herself she added, 'In fact, you haven't asked anything.'

He was silent for a moment, then he said, 'We haven't got off to a very good start, have we?'

'You can say that again,' said Siobhan tightly. As he swung the ambulance into a parking bay on the station forecourt and switched off the engine she added, 'But it looks like we're stuck with the situation so I think there are a few things we need to sort out.'

'What sort of things?' he said, staring out of the window.

'Well, you've made it pretty obvious you don't want to work with me.'

'That's not strictly true,' he muttered but he had the grace to look a little shamefaced.

'You could have fooled me,' said Siobhan crisply.

'It's not you personally—' he began.

'Maybe not,' she retorted. 'You seemed quite pleased when we first met this morning—it was only when you learned I was to be your new partner that your attitude changed.'

'Like I said, it's nothing to do with you personally,' he muttered again. 'It's difficult to explain,' he went on after a moment, 'but before I went on leave I was given to understand that Greg Freeman was to be my new partner.'

'So, did you imagine he would be any better qualified than me?' Siobhan found she had to struggle to control her rising anger. 'That my training would be somehow inferior to his?'

'Why should I think that?' A blank look came into Dave's eyes.

'Well, you didn't seem to have very much trust either in my medical judgement or in my driving skills today,' she snapped. When he didn't immediately reply she went on, 'So, if it isn't either of those, I can only conclude that it's the fact that I'm a woman that you object to.'

He sighed and gripped the steering-wheel, his knuckles showing white. 'It isn't that,' he said. 'At least, not directly. Neither does it have anything to do with your skills or your training. I would probably have been cautious of any new recruit on their first day, and that includes Greg Freeman. There's no substitute for experience, as far as I'm concerned.' He paused for a moment before going on. 'Pete Steel—he was my previous oppo—well, we worked together for years. We knew exactly what the other would do in any given circum-

stances—almost knew what each other was thinking—
so it was going to be difficult, whoever I had to work
with.'

'So why did you get so angry? I don't understand.'

He didn't answer, apparently watching as another ambulance drove into the station and parked a short distance away from them. 'I didn't like the fact that things
were changed while I was away—without my being con-
sulted,' he admitted at last.

'But it wasn't only that,' she persisted, watching as
the driver of the second ambulance, a tall, thinnish man
with cropped greying hair, climbed out of the driver's
seat.

'No,' he agreed, 'it wasn't only that. He was partly
the reason.' He nodded towards the man.

'Who is he?' asked Siobhan curiously.

'Barry Weston,' replied Dave.

'The man I was supposed to work with?'

Dave nodded. As the attendant climbed from the vehicle and came into sight, Siobhan narrowed her eyes.
'So, if that's Barry Weston, that must be Greg Freeman
with him.'

'Yes,' said Dave, 'it is. I met him this morning just
before I met you. He was parking his motorbike.'

The young man was tall and well built with very
broad shoulders.

They watched in silence as the two men made their
way into the station. Curiously, Siobhan turned to Dave.
'Is that what this is all about?' she said. 'The fact that
Greg Freeman is a well-built young man and I'm...
I'm...'

'So slight that a puff of wind might blow you away?'
He raised one eyebrow.

'That *is* it. Isn't it?' she demanded.

'Can you blame me?' He shrugged, before saying, 'Look, Siobhan, I have nothing at all against working with a woman. Let's face it, you are far prettier than Greg Freeman or dear old Pete Steel, come to that, but when it comes to lifting heavy people and manoeuvring them down steep staircases, like we had to do just now, then I'm sorry, but brawn has the edge over beauty every time.'

'You didn't even give me a chance to prove myself,' she said quickly. 'As it happens, I am very strong—but you automatically assumed I wouldn't be able to take my full share of Ivy's weight.'

'I was just being practical and realistic.' He sighed. 'I've seen it all before, you see.'

'So, why were the arrangements changed, anyway?' she asked after a moment.

He drew in his breath sharply. 'I think,' he said, 'that was the thing that got to me most—the fact that Barry Weston protests to Ted Carter and ends up yet again getting his own way.'

'What do you mean?' Siobhan stared at him, suddenly realising that this whole issue was more to do with Barry Weston than with Dave himself.

'Barry knew you'd been assigned to work with him, but he waited until I was out of the way before he went to Ted,' said Dave grimly. 'He spun Ted some yarn that his back has been playing him up lately, and that he needed someone who was the same height as himself and able to lift equally. I wouldn't have minded so much if it had been the first time this sort of thing had happened. But it isn't—not by a long chalk.' He fell silent, gazing out of the windscreen.

For a moment Siobhan couldn't think of anything further to say.

'Barry's always been something of a hypochondriac,' Dave went on at last, 'but, on the other hand, if he'd really felt he would have a problem working with someone smaller than himself he only had to come to me and say so—not wait until my back was turned, before creeping to the chief.'

There was another long silence. Siobhan threw him a glance, before taking a deep breath. 'Well,' she said slowly, 'now that we've got that straight maybe we could start again.'

She paused and, turning slightly in the cab to face Dave, said, 'I'm Siobhan O'Mara. I'm a fully trained paramedic, I have a clean driving licence, I'm used to driving heavy goods vehicles. I'm sorry I'm not very big but, I can assure you, I'll do my best to pull my weight.'

'God! You make me feel a real creep now.' Dave pulled a face, stared at her outstretched hand and then, after only a second's hesitation, grasped it firmly in his. His hand felt strong and warm. 'I'm sorry, Siobhan,' he said. 'I agree we should start again.' Without releasing her hand, he went on, 'I'm Dave Morey. I, too, am a fully trained paramedic—and I'm pleased to have you aboard.'

'Are you two going to sit there all day?'

Siobhan turned her head to find Zoe Grainger staring curiously through the window of the ambulance.

'No, Zoe,' Dave replied as, with a laugh, he finally released Siobhan's hand. 'We're just coming.'

'So it wasn't the fact that you were a woman that he objected to?' Helen stared at Siobhan across the kitchen table. It was much later that evening and the two of them had returned to The Coach House from the hospital, where they had visited Helen's father, Harry. Siobhan had been shocked and upset by her uncle's appearance and by the fact that he hadn't even recognized her. Afterwards Helen had persuaded her to join her for supper, where Siobhan had just recounted the day's events to her.

'Apparently not,' she replied. 'It seemed more to do with the fact that Barry Weston had gone behind Dave's back to the chief.'

'I have heard the ambulance crews go on about not being equally matched when it comes to lifting,' said Helen. Taking a dish of macaroni cheese from the Aga, she placed it on the kitchen table.

'Yes.' Siobhan nodded. 'I can fully understand that, just as I can understand how partners can become so used to each other over a period of time. Like Dave Morey and this…Pete Steel—is that his name?'

When Helen nodded she went on, 'They apparently worked together for years so in that respect I can see how Dave feels about working with someone new. What I couldn't understand was the sudden change in his attitude towards me.'

'What do you mean?' Helen began to serve the hot macaroni, dripping with melted cheese, onto the plates she'd put to warm on the top of the Aga.

'When we first met,' Siobhan explained, 'he seemed really pleased. He was so charming…'

'I warned you, didn't I?' said Helen drily.

'Yes, you certainly did.' Siobhan laughed. 'But the next moment he'd changed. As soon as he knew I was to be his new partner he became downright angry.'

'And you thought it was because you were a woman?'

'What was I to think?' Siobhan shrugged. 'On our very first call he treated me as if I was a complete moron, who not only had done no training but who hadn't learnt to drive either.'

'Oh, dear, you really didn't get off to a good start, did you?' Helen stared at her in amused dismay. 'What did you do?'

'I soon put him straight,' said Siobhan firmly. She helped herself to green salad from a large bowl in the centre of the table. 'I told him I was just as well trained as anyone else and that included Greg Freeman.'

'Greg Freeman?'

'The other new paramedic—the guy Dave thought was to be his new oppo—who is big and blond and just happens to be built like something out of *Baywatch*. I also let him know I've probably driven more heavy goods vehicles than he's had hot dinners.'

'Good for you,' said Helen admiringly. 'Dave Morey needs putting in his place. Just a little too sure of himself at times for my liking.'

'Yes, well.' Siobhan tucked into her supper. 'It's important to get things straight,' she said, 'right from the start.'

They were silent for a moment as they ate, then casually Helen said, 'But what did you think of him otherwise?'

'Otherwise?' Siobhan frowned. 'Oh, as a man, you mean?'

Helen nodded and, leaning across the table, refilled Siobhan's glass with the crisp white wine she had opened.

'Very attractive, actually.'

'That's what I was afraid of.'

'But you needn't worry.' Siobhan laughed. 'He's not my type.'

'Oh?'

'No, I tend to go for well-built, blond Adonis types.'

'Like Greg Freeman, you mean?'

'Now that you come to mention it—yes, I suppose you could say that.' Siobhan laughed again.

'I'm relieved to hear it.' Helen gave a deep sigh and, leaning back in her chair, sipped her wine.

CHAPTER THREE

'SO WHY the Isle of Wight?' Dave threw Siobhan a questioning glance as she negotiated the traffic around Newport's notorious Coppin's Bridge.

'Why not?' She shrugged. They were on their way back to the station, after taking a patient home from hospital.

'I just wondered, that's all,' he replied mildly. 'In my experience, most young people leave the Island to seek work, not the other way round.'

'I've always loved the Island,' she retorted, niggled by something in his manner—as if he were somehow questioning her judgement or her sanity.

'You've been here before.' It was a statement rather than a question.

'Yes, many times.' Her reply was almost flippant. 'I spent many holidays here when I was growing up—at The Coach House with Uncle Harry and Auntie Pam, and Helen,' she added as an afterthought.

'You're a close family?' There was almost a note of surprise in his voice now, as if the concept of close family life might be an alien one to him.

'Oh, yes.' Her reply was emphatic. 'And at other times they used to come to us in Ireland.'

'Are you an only child?' He'd turned his head and appeared to be studying her.

'Heavens, no. There are four of us—my three brothers and myself.'

Dave frowned. 'So where does the Isle of Wight connection come in?'

'My mother and Helen Turner are first cousins. They were born here.'

'And your father?'

'Oh, he's an Irishman through and through. My mother met him while he was working in this country. They married amidst much family opposition—from both sides, I might add.' She pulled a face and laughed. 'Later, much later,' she went on after a moment, 'when my grandfather O'Mara died my father took us all back to Ireland and he and his brother took over the family business.'

'And what is that?' asked Dave. She was aware that he'd leaned back against the window-frame and was regarding her with interest.

'Haulage,' she replied briefly. 'Heavy freight.'

'Hence your knowledge of large goods vehicles,' he said softly.

'That's right.'

'So why the paramedic bit?' He sounded really curious now, as if he found difficulty in equating the two.

Siobhan didn't answer for a moment. To Dave it must have seemed that she was intent on concentrating on the traffic, but in reality she was considering her answer. 'I always wanted to be a nurse,' she said at last, 'but I needed that added edge of excitement which I didn't think I would find on a ward. A friend suggested the paramedics so I decided to explore the possibilities.' She paused then went on, 'The more I found out the more it appealed. I also felt it was time to leave home.'

'Where exactly is home?'

'County Cork—have you ever been there?' She threw him a quick glance.

'No.' He shook his head. 'I've never been to Ireland.'

'Then you haven't truly lived,' said Siobhan, ignoring his look of amused surprise. 'County Cork must be the nearest place to heaven on this earth.'

'And yet you've chosen to leave it,' he murmured with just, she thought, a touch of cynicism in his tone.

'Ah, but I shall go back. It's always there for me to return to. But, like I said, I felt it was time to leave home for a bit. Spread my wings. Maybe see a bit of the world. Make new friends.'

'What about the friends you've left behind?'

She threw him another glance and saw the same look of amusement in his green eyes that she'd seen there when she'd first met him. It was tantalising, intriguing, but she was forced to look away quickly and concentrate once more on the road ahead when it would have been nice to linger—to see what else she could read there. 'What about them?' she said casually at last.

'Wasn't there anyone special?' he said softly.

A smile tugged at the corners of her mouth. 'They were all special,' she said at last.

By this time they had reached the station and she swung the ambulance expertly into its parking bay and switched off the engine. Before she had a chance to even open the door a second ambulance drew up alongside, with Zoe at the wheel and her partner, Josh Meecher, beside her.

'How's it going?' Zoe called as they all alighted from their vehicles.

'Fine, thanks,' Siobhan replied as the two men began some good-natured bantering and she fell into step beside Zoe.

'I've been meaning to tell you,' Zoe began as they

walked towards the station, 'we have quite a few social activities here—that is, if you are interested.'

'Oh, yes,' Siobhan replied enthusiastically. 'I am. I don't know that many people here yet and—'

'That's what I thought,' said Zoe, as Josh, who was ahead of them, pushed open the main doors of the station and held them open.

'Thanks, Josh,' Zoe said. Turning back to Siobhan, she went on, 'Well, we have the crew room here, of course, not that that's very exciting. We all belong to the social club at the Shalbrooke Hospital—they have lots of functions and activities over there. There'll be their Summer Barbeque coming up at the end of this month—that's always a bit of fun—and they have various discos and charity events which, no doubt, you'll hear all about from Dave. We'll have to see about getting membership for you.'

'Thanks,' said Siobhan. 'It all sounds fun.'

'Yes, it is,' Zoe replied. 'The other thing, of course, is the windsurfing.' As she spoke Dave looked over his shoulder and grinned.

'Windsurfing?' said Siobhan faintly, looking from one to the other.

'Oh, yes,' Zoe replied. 'There are a crowd of us—we go to a little bay near Cowes. It's great fun. Dave here is a real champ.'

Siobhan's gaze met Dave's and he inclined his head slightly. 'I don't know about that,' he said, 'but it's a great sport. You must come down and join us and see for yourself—' he broke off at that moment as the station alarm sounded and each crew hurried to collect its brief.

Siobhan and Zoe waited in Reception and only moments later they were joined again by Dave and Josh who hurried from the control room.

'It's a major incident between Yarmouth and Newport,' said Dave briefly.

They all turned and headed for the doors again.

'You'd better drive,' said Siobhan as they reached their vehicle. 'Can't risk me taking a wrong turning.' They scrambled into the ambulance and Dave started the engine. 'Do we know what it is?' asked Siobhan.

'Multi-vehicle pile-up,' he replied. 'A lorry, a mini-bus and several cars involved—many casualties.' He flicked one switch for the two-tone siren and another for the flashing blue lights.

In convoy with two other ambulances—and together with a police car—they raced to the scene of the crash. As they hurtled along the country roads Siobhan could already feel the familiar surge of adrenalin as it coursed through her veins. They could see the accident location in the distance over the tops of the hedges long before they reached the actual spot from the blue lights of the police cars and the heap of vehicles.

They drew to a halt at the side of the road, flung open the doors and, grabbing medical cases, scrambled from the vehicle. They were met by a police sergeant who briefly explained what had happened.

'The mini-bus was carrying a party of youngsters,' he said. 'It careered across the road and collided with the lorry, which was travelling in the opposite direction. Two cars then ploughed into the wreckage. The youngsters from the bus have various injuries—their driver is in a bad way. There are also injuries among the car passengers.'

'Right,' said Dave as Josh's and Zoe's vehicle squealed to a halt behind them. 'There are plenty of us. We'll see to the mini-bus people.'

The police sergeant led the way across the road to the

mini-bus, the front of which seemed to be embedded in the side of the cab of the lorry. At least a dozen teen-agers were sprawled round, some sitting in the road, cry-ing, and others in silent, shocked bewilderment.

One man, presumably the lorry driver, was sitting on the bank at the side of the road with his head in his hands, his attitude one of shocked despair. Two other policemen had apparently just succeeded in extricating the driver of the mini-bus from the tangled mass of metal and had laid him on the grass verge.

'Is he alive?' asked Siobhan, kneeling beside him.

'I don't think so,' replied one of the policemen.

'Oh, please, can you help me over here?' A young woman was kneeling beside a girl who appeared to be bleeding profusely from a wound at the side of her head. With a muttered exclamation Dave hurried across to them, leaving Siobhan to check the bus driver.

He certainly didn't appear to be breathing and already there was a bluish tinge around his lips. Pressing her fingers to the side of his neck, Siobhan searched for a pulse. She feared he was, indeed, dead but felt the faintest flutter beneath her fingers.

Quickly she snapped open her case and took out her torch. She lifted one of his closed eyelids and shone the light into his eye. Immediately the pupil reacted to the light so she knew there was life present. The first and most important thing now was to maintain an adequate airway.

Taking an endotracheal tube from her case, Siobhan removed its wrapping then introduced it into the man's mouth, at the same time checking that he was not wear-ing dentures and carefully lifting the epiglottis at the back of his throat. When intubation was complete she raced back to the ambulance and collected other equipment. On returning to the patient, she connected a ventilator to the endotracheal tube in order to administer oxygen.

The next step was to link him to a heart monitor, which showed his heart rate to be slow. A subsequent blood-pressure check also revealed a low reading so she inserted a cannula into the prominent vein in the back of the patient's hand, and had just administered a dose of atropine to increase his heart rate when she felt a movement beside her and, looking up, found Dave by her side.

'How is he?' he asked.

'I think he'll be all right,' Siobhan sat back on her heels and critically surveyed her patient. 'He has a very slow heart rate. I've just given atropine—'

They both looked up as a fire engine arrived on the scene, its klaxon wailing and lights flashing.

'A boy is trapped under one of the seats in the mini-bus,' explained Dave. 'Josh has given him Entonox to ease the pain, but the brigade lads are going to have to cut him free. I only hope his legs can be saved.'

'What about the girl?' asked Siobhan, glancing across the road.

'I've managed to staunch the bleeding,' Dave replied, 'and I've put up a line to keep a vein open, but only as a precaution, and with a very slow drip because she has a serious head injury.' He stood up. 'I'd better get back and see to someone else. There are a lot of superficial injuries.' He stopped as the man on the ground began groaning.

'I'm going to give him a shot for his pain,' Siobhan took an ampoule from her case and fitted it to the cannula in the man's hand.

'He's arrested!' said Dave suddenly. 'I'll massage—you get the defib.' He sank to his knees beside the man.

Siobhan scrambled to her feet and sped to the back of the ambulance where she collected the defibrillator, then raced back to the man on the ground.

Dave had already commenced heart massage which he continued while she set up the machine. Then, as if they'd worked together for a lifetime, they automatically swung into the carefully rehearsed routine of massage, shock and resuscitation.

For a time there was no sign of a response and it seemed they would be unsuccessful, but after the second attempt the monitor began to flicker and the signs of life were present once more.

'He's with us,' muttered Dave. 'I think the sooner we can get him aboard and into the Shalbrooke the better. We'll take the girl with the head injury as well.'

Siobhan nodded and, while keeping a close watch on the patient for any further signs of heart failure, she began to pack up her equipment in readiness to move him to the ambulance.

Within minutes Dave returned with a stretcher and together they lifted the man, carried him to the ambulance and settled him on one of the two couches.

'You stay with him,' Dave said. 'I'll go and get the girl.'

'How will you manage?' she asked.

'I'll get one of the policemen to help,' said Dave shortly.

Moments later he and a policeman were back, carrying the girl on a stretcher between them and accompanied by the woman whom Siobhan had seen earlier trying to help the girl.

'The lady's going to travel with us,' said Dave as they lowered the girl onto the second couch.

'Do you want me to drive?' asked Siobhan, fully expecting Dave to say yes, not for one moment imagining that he would trust her to remain in the back.

'No,'' he said briefly. 'I'll drive. That is, if you're quite happy to attend.'

'Of course,' she replied coolly. Briefly her eyes met his as he jumped from the back of the ambulance and fastened the doors. She was alone, with a woman in shock and two badly injured patients.

'We were on holiday.' The woman's voice was barely more than a whisper.

'Sorry?' Siobhan could hardly hear her as Dave started the engine.

'On holiday…' the woman repeated. 'Church youth group…staying at a holiday village…' Her gaze flickered to the man on the other couch. 'Is he…? Is he…?' she began fearfully.

'No.' Siobhan checked the monitor and shook her head. 'No, he isn't dead. We think he had a heart attack.' She leaned over to adjust the ventilator.

'Who is he?' she added after a moment.

'He's our vicar,' said the woman. 'He organised this trip. Oh, do you think he'll be all right?'

'We hope so,' said Siobhan. 'There's every chance he will be once we get him to hospital. What's his name?' she asked after a moment.

'Colin,' the woman replied. 'The Reverend Colin Appleby.'

'And you?' said Siobhan. 'Who are you?'

'Ruth Symmonds—I'm a youth worker.'

The girl on the couch began to moan and they both turned to look at her.

'That's Angela,' said the woman. 'Angela Barnes—she's only thirteen. Oh, whatever am I going to tell her mother?' Her voice caught in her throat.

With a quick look at the Reverend Appleby Siobhan moved across the gangway to check on Angela.

She had suffered a severe blow to her head and her hair was matted with blood which had run down her face. A closer inspection showed Siobhan that the blood was already seeping through the dressing pad that Dave had secured over the wound. She took a fresh pad from her case, removed the first one and applied the second, pressing it firmly against the wound in a further attempt to staunch the bleeding.

Even as she sat beside the girl, Colin Appleby began muttering and started trying to pull out the endotracheal tube.

'Oh, no,' Ruth Symmonds gasped. 'Look at Colin. Oh, dear, what shall I do?'

'Come here,' said Siobhan calmly, 'and hold this in place.' She surprised herself at the degree of authority in her voice.

Meekly Ruth Symmonds did as she was told.

'Now hold it firmly,' said Siobhan. 'That's right—like that. The pressure should stop any further bleeding.'

Moving across the narrow gangway, she adjusted Colin Appleby's airway. 'It's all right, Colin,' she said in the same calm tones. 'Keep this in place—it's helping you to breathe. We'll soon have you at hospital and they'll give you something else for the pain.'

Something in her tone or her actions must have calmed the man because he stopped struggling and moaning and lay quietly.

'Everything OK back there?' called Dave from the front.

'Yes, fine, thanks,' Siobhan replied.

'Good—we're approaching the Shalbrooke now—they're ready to receive us.'

As the doors were finally thrown open, a doctor climbed into the back of the ambulance and immediately checked on Colin Appleby's condition.

Siobhan gave a brief report as first Colin and then Angela were lifted out of the vehicle and received by the waiting staff. Accompanied by Dave, they were whisked away on trolleys into the A and E department, leaving Siobhan with Ruth.

As they stepped down from the ambulance the other two vehicles sped into the car park, their blue lights flashing but their sirens silent now in the grounds of the hospital. Other staff moved forward, Helen and Georgina Merrick among them, and yet more of the injured were taken from the ambulances and wheeled inside.

'What do you think I should do?' asked Ruth Symmonds.

'Give your name at the desk,' said Siobhan. 'Explain who you are. I'm sure they'll let you stay until there's further news of Angela. I say, are you all right?' she added anxiously as the woman suddenly went very white and appeared to sway slightly.

'Yes… I just feel a bit faint, that's all…' Ruth replied shakily.

'You're not hurt, are you?' asked Siobhan.

'Not really.' Ruth paused. 'It's only my arm.'

'What about your arm?' asked Siobhan.

'It hurts.' Ruth sank down onto a nearby chair. 'I think I may have broken it…'

Siobhan looked in disbelief at the woman's arm. It appeared to be hanging by her side at a very unnatural angle. 'Why ever didn't you say?' she said.

'You had quite enough to be getting on with,' said Ruth, biting her lip with pain, 'without having to be worried about me.'

'Stay there,' said Siobhan. 'I'll tell someone.' She looked round the crowded reception area, at the patients waiting for treatment and at the frantically busy staff—and was just wondering who she could ask when Helen came out of one of the treatment rooms.

'Helen,' Siobhan called, starting forward.

'What is it?' It was obvious that Helen was in a great hurry as the hospital procedures to deal with a large RTA got under way.

'The lady over there in the chair.' Siobhan pointed to Ruth. 'She came in my ambulance with the girl, Angela Barnes, but she's only just told me she's injured her arm—it looks like a fracture.'

'I see,' said Helen. 'We'll have to get her into X-Ray.' She paused. 'You say she was with Angela Barnes?' When Siobhan nodded she said, 'Is she a relative, do you know?'

'No, I don't think so. She said she's a youth worker. They were on a holiday trip.'

'Oh. Only...'

'Is the girl all right?' asked Siobhan quickly. There was something in Helen's manner that made her wonder.

'She looks to be in a bad way,' Helen replied briefly. 'But don't worry, Siobhan. I'll get someone to see to that lady—what's her name?'

'Ruth,' said Siobhan. 'Ruth Symmonds.'

She watched as Helen called a nurse, who hurried across to Ruth. She was about to turn away to go back to the car park when Dave came out of the treatment room with Josh.

'Do we have to go back?' she said.

'No.' Dave shook his head. 'Josh and Zoe are going back, but that's all that'll be needed.' He threw her a quick glance. 'You all right?' he said.

'Yes,' she nodded. 'I think so—a bit stunned.'

'Well, it was a bit hairy back there.'

'Oh, I didn't mean that,' said Siobhan quickly, not wanting him to think she hadn't been able to cope. 'It was that woman, Ruth.'

'What about her?' asked Dave as he pushed open the glass doors.

'Well, she never said a word—about being injured, I mean—all the time in the ambulance. She even helped with Angela. But she didn't say anything until we got into Reception.'

'And was she? Injured?' Dave frowned.

Siobhan nodded. 'It looks like she has a fractured arm. She must have been in agony, but she was so quiet...'

'That's very often the way,' said Dave.

Slowly they walked back to their vehicle and climbed into the back where they began to tidy up, replacing the stretchers, blankets and equipment.

'The girl's in a bad way,' said Dave after a moment.

'Yes.' Siobhan nodded. 'Helen said so.' She threw him a quick glance and saw that he looked genuinely upset.

'She took a turn for the worse as we got her into the treatment room,' he added. 'Didn't look as if she was going to make it.'

They were silent for a moment. Quietly, Dave said, 'You did well back there, especially with the driver.'

'Thanks,' said Siobhan. Suddenly she felt weary but at the same time ridiculously pleased that he had complimented her.

'At least you showed that you can keep a cool head,'

Dave went on. He paused. 'Was that your first big traffic accident?'

'Of course not,' she replied indignantly. 'We have traffic in Ireland as well, you know—even in County Cork.'

He grinned. 'Really?'

'Yes.' She felt her colour rising. 'And aren't you forgetting where I did my training? I attended several RTAs in London.' She was on the defensive again, desperate that he shouldn't think her inexperienced or lacking in training procedures in any way.

'OK.' He lifted his hands in a defensive gesture. 'I just wondered, that's all, especially...' He shrugged and trailed off.

'Especially what?' She stopped what she was doing and stared at him.

'Nothing...' He turned away.

'No. I want to know,' she demanded. 'What did you mean?'

'Well, if you must know, I was rather surprised that you didn't wear gloves.'

She stared at him.

'Maybe you don't bother.' He shrugged. 'But, be warned, in this division it's something Ted Carter is very particular about, especially these days, with AIDS...'

'But I do.' She swallowed. How could she have been so stupid? 'Usually, I do.'

'But not today?' Dave raised one eyebrow, the gesture both knowing and maddening. He knew full well she had forgotten. 'An oversight, maybe?'

She took a deep breath. There was no point denying it. 'Yes, an oversight,' she admitted.

'Never mind.' He jumped from the back of the ambulance and stood for a moment, looking up at her. 'I doubt you have too much to worry about with the Reverend and young Angela.'

She made to jump and he held out his hand to steady her. She wanted to refuse it but somehow that would have seemed downright petty. His hand was firm, his arm strong and steady. 'I don't know what you are implying,' she said, as she withdrew her hand smartly.

He frowned. 'I'm not implying anything.'

'It sounded to me as if you were making assumptions about lifestyles,' she said crisply, 'and that is something, in my training at least, I was taught never to do.'

'No, love,' said Dave, the expression in his eyes hardening, becoming opaque, 'not at all. I was merely being practical and, I'd hoped, reassuring. Obviously I was wrong.'

With that he swung away from her and walked round to the driver's seat.

Siobhan bit her lip as she walked to the passenger side. Somehow she felt she'd got it wrong again where Dave was concerned. Back there at the RTA they had worked well together, with the friction of the previous day apparently forgotten. Now, because of her stupidity over the gloves, they seemed to be at odds again.

CHAPTER FOUR

SIOBHAN'S shift didn't end until late that evening and when she got back to The Coach House it was to find that Helen was already home. Her car was parked in its usual place alongside the house, but on the drive in front of the entrance was a dark blue estate car.

Fleetingly Siobhan wondered who it belonged to. Assuming that Helen was entertaining, she parked her Mini and was about to climb the stairs to the stable flat when Helen's front door opened and Chester loped across the yard to greet her, his tail wagging furiously.

'Hello, Chester.' Siobhan bent to pat the dog's head and when she looked up again it was to find Helen standing on the doorstep with a man.

'Siobhan,' she called, 'come over—there's someone I'd like you to meet.'

Slowly Siobhan made her way across the forecourt, Chester padding silently by her side. It was the end of what had been a long and, at times, difficult day. She felt hot, scruffy and tired, in need of a shower, a change of clothes and a meal. The last thing she wanted was to be meeting someone for the first time.

The man was tall and fairly burly, with dark, receding hair. As Siobhan approached she noticed he was watching her with interest.

'Siobhan, this is Richard Fleetwood,' said Helen. 'Richard, this is my cousin, Siobhan O'Mara. Richard is senior partner at the medical centre in Shalbrooke,' she added by way of explanation.

'Hello, Siobhan.' Her hand was grasped in a firm handshake. 'I've heard a lot about you.'

'Oh, dear,' she said. 'How dreadful for you.'

'On the contrary,' he said, 'I've heard nothing but good. Helen tells me you've joined the paramedics, which means we shall see quite a bit of you. Welcome to the Isle of Wight,' he added. 'I hope you'll be happy with us.'

'Thank you,' Siobhan smiled, on a first impression instinctively liking him.

'I'd better be on my way, Helen.' Richard Fleetwood half turned to Helen and, to Siobhan's amazement, kissed her lightly on the mouth.

They watched as he climbed into his car, reversed and with a wave of his hand drove away.

'Are all Island GPs that friendly?' asked Siobhan with a chuckle.

'Richard and I are old friends,' said Helen. She spoke coolly, but Siobhan was amused to see that her cheeks had grown quite pink. She hadn't realised there was a man in Helen's life, but she was delighted to find that might be the case. She knew her mother had long despaired over Helen finding the right man and getting married.

'So it would seem,' she said. When it was obvious that Helen wasn't about to volunteer any further information she went on, 'Oh, well, I suppose I'd better go and sort myself out—it's been quite a day one way and another.' She turned to go.

'Oh, Siobhan,' said Helen suddenly.

'Yes?' She paused, wondering at the change in Helen's tone.

'The girl, Angela Barnes—I'm afraid she didn't make it.'

Siobhan stared at Helen in dismay. 'What happened?'

'She suffered a massive brain haemorrhage and died late this afternoon.'

'Poor girl.' Siobhan bit her lip. 'What about the others?' she asked after a moment. 'The vicar and Ruth Symmonds—do you know what happened to them?'

'The vicar was all right, as far as I know,' Helen replied. 'He was transferred to the coronary care unit and the woman, Ruth—well, you were quite right. She had fractured her ulna in two places, as it happened. She had her arm set and she sat with Angela until she died. Of the others, one boy had a foot amputated and another had serious head injuries. The lorry driver was all right, but two of the people in the cars also sustained serious injuries.'

'It was quite an accident, wasn't it?' said Siobhan.

'By Island standards, yes, it was,' said Helen. 'I dare say it was by your standards as well, wasn't it? I imagine traffic conditions in Cork are similar to ours.'

'Don't you start,' said Siobhan. 'I've had enough of that from Dave Morey.'

'Is he giving you a hard time?' Helen frowned.

'No, not really.'

'I just wondered, that's all,' said Helen slowly. 'There was all that yesterday about his working with you, and now...'

'Don't worry,' said Siobhan shortly. 'There isn't anything I can't handle. Believe it or not,' she added after a moment, 'he actually complimented me after today's call.'

'Did he?' said Helen, a slightly cynical note in her voice. 'That was big of him.'

'Yes, he told me I'd done well and kept very calm.'

'Well, I suppose he didn't have to.'

'True, but then he bawled me out for forgetting to put surgical gloves on for the RTA.'

'Oh, dear,' said Helen.

'That was my own fault,' said Siobhan. 'I just couldn't believe I'd been so stupid. I was so intent on resuscitating the Reverend Appleby that I forgot everything else.'

'Well, I'm sure the Reverend will be eternally grateful to you,' said Helen with a smile.

'Let's hope so. It certainly hasn't done much to improve my working relationship with my partner,' said Siobhan drily.

'And there was me, worrying that you would be having to fight off his advances.' Helen gave a short laugh.

'No fear of that. I doubt he can stand the sight of me.'

'Have you made friends with anyone else?' asked Helen, a slight note of anxiety in her voice.

'Yes…a girl called Zoe Grainger. Do you know her?'

'Oh, yes,' said Helen. 'I know Zoe.'

Siobhan threw Helen a quick glance, but her face was expressionless. 'Well,' she went on, 'she's going to introduce me to the hospital social club and arrange membership for me. Oh, and she said something about a group of them who go to the beach at weekends for windsurfing. Do you know anything about that?'

'A lot of the younger ones go,' said Helen. 'Hospital staff, paramedics and staff from the med centre. I know that much, but I'm afraid it isn't exactly my scene so I can't tell you a lot more. Are you going to go?'

'Yes,' said Siobhan. 'I thought I might give it a try at the weekend.'

'Good,' said Helen. 'I'm glad to hear it. I would hate to think of you moping about here all the time on your own. You need to get out with people of your own age.'

* * *

The rest of Siobhan's first week seemed to be taken up with routine hospital admissions and discharges, with none of the drama and excitement of those first two days.

'That's the way it goes,' said Dave when she commented on the fact. 'Sometimes it's quiet for days on end, but you'll find the further we go into the summer the more drama there will be.'

'Is that how you like it?' she asked, casting him a sidelong glance. They were on their way to transfer an elderly cancer patient to the day centre at the local hospice.

He shrugged. 'I don't mind, although I must admit I do prefer to be busy. On the other hand, you can overdose on drama. These days I think I'd settle for the quiet life, given the choice.'

'You surprise me.' Siobhan raised her eyebrows. 'I would have thought you would prefer to be where the action is.'

He laughed. 'You forget I've been at this lark a lot longer than you have.'

'You mean you've seen it all and done it all?'

'Something like that. I don't think there's much Pete and I haven't had to deal with.'

She saw his mouth tighten slightly and recalled what Helen had told her when she'd first arrived.

'I understand he was forced to take retirement on medical grounds.'

'That's right.' Dave's reply was abrupt, then he added briefly, 'He has MS.'

'That's tragic,' she said. 'How old is he?'

'Early thirties, that's all. And a family man—two young boys. I still get angry whenever I think of it. It just all seems so unfair...'

They were silent as they approached Cowes and

headed for the seafront, then she said, 'Have you ever been married?'

'Good Lord, no.' He shot her a startled glance, taking his eyes briefly from the road. With a muttered exclamation he had to swerve to straighten the vehicle.

'Would that be such a terrible prospect?' she asked mildly.

'For me, probably, yes,' he replied. 'I came to the conclusion years ago that I'm quite simply not the marrying kind. The thought of responsibilities—a mortgage, kids, that sort of thing—just makes my blood run cold.'

'One assumes there must be another side—to marriage, I mean—otherwise no one would ever undertake it,' she replied carefully.

'Oh, undoubtedly, there must be.' He paused and gave a wicked chuckle. 'I'm damned if I can see what it is, though. In my experience, if you're clever enough you can have those benefits without the responsibilities.'

Siobhan was saved from answering as he brought the ambulance to a halt before an apartment block, and they were both compelled once more to give their attention to the job in hand.

The patient was an elderly lady who, as Dave had previously explained, had been suffering from the effects of cancer for many years. She had received courses of chemotherapy and radiotherapy during the long years of her treatment which had all left their mark on her ravaged body. In spite of all this, nothing seemed to have reduced her will to live or quenched her indomitable spirit.

'Hello, Lily.' Dave greeted her like an old friend. 'How are we this morning?'

'I don't know about you, young man,' she replied tartly, 'but I'm very well—taking everything into ac-

count. Who's this?' she asked, her gaze falling on
Siobhan.

'She's my new oppo, Lily,' said Dave, as he opened
the folding chair he was carrying. 'Her name's Siobhan.'

'Irish?' Lily eyed Siobhan speculatively and then, not
giving her a chance to reply, said, 'Yes, I can see you
are with that colouring.' Looking up at Dave again, she
went on, 'Pete's had to give up, has he?'

'Afraid so,' said Dave.

'Poor lad,' said Lily. 'I saw his wife, Sue, last
week—tried to persuade her to take him to Lourdes.'

'Not sure they'd be able to do any more for him,' said
Dave.

'Not for his poor body, maybe,' Lily replied.

'I've been to Lourdes,' said Siobhan quietly, as she
tucked a blanket round Lily's knees.

Dave shot her a startled glance. 'Whatever for?'

'Oh, not as a patient,' she replied quickly. 'I went with
a group of handicapped children from County Cork.'

'Then you will know what I mean,' said Lily, eyeing
her shrewdly.

Siobhan nodded. 'Yes,' she said. 'I know exactly what
you mean.'

'Lily goes every year, don't you, Lily?' said Dave
cheerfully. 'Still waiting for that miracle cure, aren't
you, love?'

Siobhan's eyes met Lily's over the top of Dave's head
as he bent to lift her chair.

Carefully they carried Lily out of the building and into
the waiting ambulance. As Dave climbed into the cab
Siobhan sat beside Lily as they travelled to the hospice.
They'd only gone a short distance when Siobhan realised
the old lady was watching her with barely concealed
curiosity.

'You remind me of someone,' she said bluntly at last, 'but I'm blessed if I can think who it is— Wait a minute.' Her frown deepened. 'Yes, I can. It's a girl I used to teach—her name was Jennifer, Jennifer Cooper.'

Siobhan smiled. 'Jennifer Cooper is my mother,' she said. 'Except that her name is Jennifer O'Mara now.'

'I knew it,' said Lily triumphantly. 'You're the image of her—apart from your red hair, of course. Jennifer was dark but your eyes are the same as hers and the shape of your face...and your smile,' she added. 'But not that hair...nor your pale complexion.'

'My colouring is my father's,' said Siobhan. 'All the O'Maras have red hair.' As she was speaking she knew with a sudden certainty that from the driver's seat Dave was listening to every word they were saying.

'Your mother came from a very old Isle of Wight family,' said Lily. 'How has she coped with life in Ireland?'

'Very well,' said Siobhan. 'I think at times she gets homesick, but when it comes to the way of life the two aren't so very different.'

'I know,' said Lily. 'My mother was Irish.'

'Ah,' said Siobhan.

'So, what about you?' asked Lily after a moment.

'Me?' said Siobhan.

'Yes, how will you cope?'

'Oh, I don't doubt I shall cope very well,' replied Siobhan firmly. 'Like I said, it's not that different.'

'I didn't mean the way of life,' said Lily crisply. 'I meant, with that young heathen of a partner you have.'

There came a guffaw of laughter from the cab, which confirmed Siobhan's suspicions that Dave was indeed listening, but once again she was saved from answering as he said, 'She can't believe her good fortune, Lily, in being the one chosen to work alongside me.'

Lily's snort of indignation was clearly audible as Dave brought the ambulance to a halt at the front entrance of the hospice.

'We'll be back for you later, Lily,' said Dave moments later as they carefully handed her over into the care of the hospice staff.

'Don't come too early,' said Lily. 'We're having a bridge match today. Reginald and I are through to the finals.'

They were still chuckling when they returned to the ambulance and shut the doors. 'She's incredible,' said Dave. 'I really don't know how she keeps going or where she gets her determination from.'

'There's nothing stronger than the will to survive,' said Siobhan quietly as she slipped into the passenger seat beside him.

'Maybe not,' he replied, 'but even that must wear a bit thin sometimes when the odds are so heavily stacked. Speaking of which…' he glanced at his wristwatch '…I just want to pop into Pete's on the way back. It's his nipper's birthday—I've got a card to deliver.'

A little later they stopped before a red-bricked semi and Dave ran inside. Siobhan found herself leaning forward and watching with interest as, in response to his ring at the doorbell, a slim, dark-haired woman answered the door. After greeting Dave, her gaze moved automatically to the ambulance. No doubt she was curious to see who had replaced her husband as Dave's partner.

Even as the thought crossed Siobhan's mind she found herself sitting back, out of the woman's line of vision. Suddenly she felt guilty just for being there, which was ridiculous because Pete Steel's affliction was nothing whatsoever to do with her.

The next time she looked Dave was no longer in sight, although the front door was still open. Minutes later he strode down the path and wrenched open the door, his face set and unsmiling. Clambering aboard, he started the engine without so much as a backward glance.

As they drew away Siobhan felt her gaze instinctively drawn towards the house. The front door was tightly closed now and there was no sign of Pete Steel's wife, but as they passed the house she saw in the large picture window, the unmistakable outline of a man sitting in a chair, a man who watched them as they drove away.

Apprehensively she glanced at Dave but his expression was still set, his jaw tight. He must have sensed her interest, however, and a moment later he appeared to almost explode as he released his pent-up emotion.

'It's so bloody cruel!'

'Yes,' she agreed quietly, 'it is. I can understand how you must feel.'

'No, you can't,' he snarled. 'How can you? No one knows.'

She didn't answer. At last he sighed. 'Sorry,' he said. 'I didn't mean that. It isn't your fault.'

'That's OK,' she said. 'It must seem like it's my fault at times, what with me having taken his job...'

'I just feel so helpless,' he said. 'We've been mates for years, but I feel so frustrated. He rejects everything I suggest. Poor Sue is at her wit's end with him. He just sits in that chair all day, staring out of the window.'

'It's early days yet,' said Siobhan slowly. 'There's bound to be a period of adjustment—probably more mentally than physically. I've done quite a lot of work with handicapped people,' she added quickly, afraid he would accuse her again of not knowing what she was talking about.

This time, however, he didn't say anything, and they drove back to the station in silence. They were just entering the grounds when Siobhan said, 'What were Pete's hobbies? Before, I mean.'

'Football and windsurfing,' Dave replied shortly, 'both of which could prove a bit difficult now, I would imagine.'

'Nothing else?' She frowned.

'No, not really.' He paused fractionally, then went on, 'Only our disco work.'

'So, what's that all about?' asked Siobhan curiously.

'It goes back a long way.' Dave switched off the engine, but made no attempt to get out of the cab. He must have sensed her curiosity for he went on, 'It started one night at the hospital social club when the DJ didn't turn up and Pete and I took over. They must have liked us because the next function they had they asked us to do the honours again. We donated the fee towards the appeal for a kidney machine and, well, the whole thing just snowballed from there. It became automatically assumed we'd do every event. Now, I'm not sure what will happen…'

'But surely there's no reason why Pete can't do that?'

'Well, I wouldn't have thought so,' said Dave with a shrug, 'but he's said he isn't interested. That he doesn't want to do it any more. So, you can see what we're up against.'

'Maybe he'll have another think about that,' said Siobhan, 'when he's had time to come to terms with things a bit more.'

'Yes, maybe,' said Dave, but he didn't sound too optimistic.

They left the ambulance and went back into the station. All was quiet so they made their way to the crew room.

Barry Weston and Greg Freeman were there, drinking coffee. Siobhan poured herself a coffee from the machine and automatically poured one for Dave.

'Nice to have a little woman to wait on you, isn't it?' called Barry Weston sarcastically as they both sat down.

'Just think, Barry,' Dave replied smoothly. 'That privilege could have been yours.'

Siobhan looked swiftly from one to the other. She hoped they weren't about to have an argument. It seemed the issue of Barry going to the chief behind Dave's back was still far from resolved. In an attempt to avert any further friction she looked at Greg. 'How's it going?' she asked.

'Not so bad,' Greg nodded. 'What about you?'

'Yes, fine, thanks. I'm enjoying it.'

'Give her a month and she'll be as sick of it all as the rest of us,' sneered Barry. 'When she's pulled a few muscles, put her back out—'

'Shut up, Barry,' said Dave. 'Not everyone is such a whinger as you. Although you might find this hard to believe, there are some who enjoy the job.'

'Actually, I enjoy it,' said Greg. For a moment he looked puzzled and Siobhan found herself wondering if he'd even known about all the argument that had gone on over who should work with who. The fact that Dave had actually stuck up for her had also surprised her— and to Barry Weston, of all people.

She settled down in her chair and had barely had the chance to take as much as a sip of her coffee when the alarm bell sounded.

'That's us,' said Greg, jumping to his feet.

Barry Weston muttered an oath under his breath and drained his own mug before getting to his feet. Without so much as a further glance at Dave or Siobhan, he strolled from the crew room.

Greg paused at the door. 'See you guys later,' he said, with his quick, shy smile.

'Yes, see you, Greg,' said Dave. As the door swung shut behind him Dave gave a deep sigh. 'He's got a serious attitude problem,' he muttered staring into the depths of his mug.

'Who, Greg Freeman?' asked Siobhan with a faint grin.

'No, of course not. Barry Weston.'

'Oh, him.' She said it with a dismissive gesture, as if Barry's attitude would be the last thing she would allow to bother her.

Dave was silent for a moment, before saying with a sigh, 'You're right. He's not worth wasting time over. Life's too short.' He paused. 'It's funny, though, we've never really seen eye to eye, you know.'

'Have you worked together for long?' asked Siobhan.

'Long enough.' Dave pulled a face. 'But it goes back further than that. He used to live in the same road as me when I was a kid. He didn't like me then, any more than I liked him.'

'Any particular reason?' Siobhan took another sip of her coffee.

'He was always hanging around my sister,' muttered Dave. 'She couldn't stand him either.'

'Ah,' said Siobhan. 'So where's your sister now?'

'She lives on the mainland.'

'Do you still live in the same road?' Quite suddenly, for some reason which she was at a loss to explain, she wanted to know more. He knew quite a bit about her now but she knew virtually nothing of him, apart from the fact that he wasn't married and believed himself to be not the marrying kind.

'No,' he replied. 'Like I said, that was when I was a kid.'

'Where was that?'

'In Newport.'

'And where do you live now?'

'Still in Newport.' He took another mouthful of coffee.

'With your parents?'

'They're both dead,' he said quietly.

'Oh, I'm sorry.' Suddenly she wished she hadn't asked.

'It's OK.' He shrugged. 'It was some time ago now.'

'Even so.' Siobhan frowned. She couldn't imagine life without her own parents, without the closeness of family life.

'My dad died first,' Dave added unexpectedly. 'A coronary—very sudden it was. I shall always believe the shock of it killed my mother.'

'They must have been very close,' said Siobhan gently.

'That's the strange part,' said Dave thoughtfully. 'I never thought of them as being particularly close and neither did anyone else. They used to argue a lot, you see. But I suppose they must have been close because when the end came...' He trailed off, once again staring moodily into the depths of his mug. 'You never know, do you,' he said after a while, 'just what goes on within a marriage?'

Siobhan shook her head. 'No. I suppose not. It's a bit different with my parents, though...'

'How do you mean?' He threw her an interested glance.

'They are besotted with each other. Still, after all this time. It was apparently love at first sight, and they still feel the same way all these years later.' She paused. 'Maybe it was like that for your parents as well, except that—'

'They had a funny way of showing it!' With a laugh he finished the sentence for her. 'But, yes, you could be right. Maybe it was like that. I guess I'll never know for sure.'

When he fell silent she asked, 'So, where do you live now?'

'Like I say, still in Newport. But not in the old back street terrace where I was brought up. Now I have one of those smart new flats down by the quay. Gone up in the world, as my gran would have said.'

Siobhan smiled. 'Would your parents have been proud of that?'

He reflected for a moment before answering. 'Mum would have been,' he said at last. 'She was all for folk trying to better themselves.'

'And your dad?' Siobhan prompted when he fell silent.

'Dad?' He gave his amused grin. 'Dad would have said, ''Don't go getting above yourself, nipper''.'

They were both laughing when the door opened and Zoe and Josh came into the room. Zoe glanced from one to the other of them and raised her eyebrows, as if to question the cause of their laughter, but before she had a chance to comment the alarm went off yet again and they both scrambled to their feet.

'Come on, kid,' said Dave, and this time there was an unmistakable note of affection in his tone. 'That's our shout.'

CHAPTER FIVE

IT WAS Sunday morning, and Siobhan had that good-to-be-alive feeling. It was a warm, sunny, June day which stretched gloriously before her. She had already decided she would take Zoe Grainger up on her offer and join the others down at the beach.

'Want to come with me?' she called to Helen as she stowed her beach gear in the boot of her Mini.

Helen, who was weeding the deep herbaceous border at the side of the house, sat back on her heels and pushed her hair out of her eyes. 'No, thanks.' She smiled. 'Like I said, it's not really my scene—all that activity.'

'What you're doing looks pretty energetic,' Siobhan observed.

'I find it very therapeutic,' Helen replied, 'which I very much doubt I would with windsurfing. That, for me, would be extremely stressful.'

'You could always just sit on the beach in the sun and watch or read a book.'

'No, honestly, Siobhan,' Helen said. 'Don't worry about me. I shall be fine. When I've finished this I shall go and see Dad, then later I'm going out to lunch...'

'With Richard?' Siobhan raised her eyebrows.

'Yes, with Richard,' Helen admitted. 'It's a standing arrangement for Sundays. Either he joins me—and Dad, when he's well enough—or I go to Richard's house at Newtown Creek and join him and his children.'

'His children?' said Siobhan, faintly startled, wondering for one moment if Richard Fleetwood wasn't quite what she had imagined.

'Yes, Cassie and Alex,' said Helen. She must have noticed Siobhan's expression for she expanded, 'Richard is a widower—his wife died some years ago. She was a friend of mine. I used to go to Newton for Sunday lunch when she was alive—we're just keeping up a tradition.'

'That's nice,' said Siobhan, thinking it really sounded rather dull. She hoped it wasn't, for Helen's sake. 'Well, if you're sure I can't persuade you otherwise,' she said, 'I'd better be getting along.'

'Take care, won't you?' said Helen. 'Don't want you in A and E with any fractured limbs.'

'Oh, don't worry,' Siobhan laughed. 'I'll be careful—and I certainly won't be taking any risks. See you later.' With a wave of her hand, she got into her car and drove smartly away down the drive.

She knew the general direction of the cove where Zoe had told her they congregated at weekends, but in spite of that she took a couple of wrong turnings before at last she found herself on a quiet road at the top of a long grassy slope that ran right down to the beach.

She guessed she'd found the right spot because of the group of parked cars. All had roof-racks for transporting surfing equipment, and among them she recognized both Dave's and Josh's cars.

Getting out of her car she stood for a while, taking in great lungfuls of the heady bracing air and shading her eyes from the bright sunlight which glistened achingly on the sea.

All was still, the only sounds the cries of seagulls as they dived and swooped and the distant noise of shipping in the Solent. The sun was warm on her bare legs and across her shoulders through the thin cotton of the white shirt she wore knotted above her midriff.

The beach was hidden from her view, tucked in beneath the grassy slope, but the stretch of inshore water was deserted save for three orange marker-buoys that bobbed up and down on the surface.

And then she saw them, like a trail of fireflies skimming over the surface of the waves driven by a brisk coastal breeze—tiny figures perfectly balanced on narrow boards clinging to sails as thin as gossamer as they tacked and gybed in the path of the sun.

Siobhan's breath caught in her throat as a tingle of excitement rippled down her spine. She watched for a few moments, then pulled her beach-bag from the boot of the Mini and hurried forward down the slope, her steps growing shorter and faster as it became steeper and she neared the end.

There were trees at the base of the slope and as Siobhan came through these and into the cove she was surprised to find there were also several huts which hadn't been visible from the road. One was a small café with white tables and chairs outside and others looked like changing huts, while the largest was loaded with windsurfing equipment and looked as if it could be some sort of club headquarters.

There were a fair number of people in the cove—some in the largest hut, talking loudly, others sitting outside the café, enjoying the sunshine, while others sat on the sea wall, cheering as the first of the line of windsurfers skimmed through the waves and up onto the beach.

No one seemed to notice Siobhan as she made her way down the stony path and into the cove, where she sat down on a clump of rocks and joined the onlookers.

She saw Zoe return, wearing a black wetsuit with fluorescent green stripes, followed by Josh, then two others—a girl and a man whom she didn't recognise—and, finally, Dave Morey skimmed to a halt on the beach.

He didn't notice her sitting quietly there on the rocks so she was able to watch him unobserved. His black hair was wet and glistened in the sun. He was laughing as he slipped from his board—possibly at something that one of the others had said. His head was thrown back, his teeth gleaming white against the brown of his skin.

Siobhan couldn't fail to notice how relaxed and happy he looked and, for that matter, how handsome, she thought with a little shock. She'd thought him attractive before, but not necessarily handsome. There couldn't, however, be any denying that fact now, especially when he began to peel off his wetsuit, revealing the hard, muscular body beneath.

He must have sensed someone watching him for quite suddenly he paused, glanced up and looked straight into her eyes. She saw his shock at seeing her there, a shock which was quickly replaced by pleasure and then, as she stood up, by admiration as his gaze roamed over her, taking in every detail—from her mass of hair, loose today and untamed, to her bare limbs and midriff, her shorts and the crisp, white shirt she wore.

Stepping right out of his wetsuit and leaving it on the beach—clad only now in the briefest of shorts—he covered the distance between them in a few easy strides.

'Hello,' he said softly, his gaze not leaving hers for one second. 'This is a surprise.'

'Hello, Dave,' she replied, wondering why her heart was pounding quite so hard and afraid he might be able to hear it. 'Zoe suggested I come down here—I see she's over there,' she added, without looking.

'Yes.' He nodded, also without looking.

It was as if neither could look away from the other. Which, when you thought about it, Siobhan decided, was rather ridiculous, considering how much time they'd spent together during the previous week and had remained comparatively indifferent to each other.

But that had been different, quite different. For Dave at work, in his paramedic gear, was very different from this Dave, with his sun-bronzed body, hard, lean thighs and, above all, with that expression in those fascinating green eyes as he looked at her.

They might have gone on gazing at each other for ever, but that was something they would never know for at that moment there came a shout from the water's edge as someone called Siobhan's name. Somehow she finally managed to tear her gaze away, to find that Zoe had just discovered her presence and was walking towards them.

'Siobhan—you made it!' she cried. 'Well done. Now, where would you like to sit? The wind is good offshore this morning so there will be plenty of activity for you to watch. I can't imagine those rocks are too comfortable,' she went on, 'so how about moving to outside the café? There are usually some of the gang sitting out so you shouldn't get lonely. On the other hand, maybe you'd prefer to simply soak up the sun. I wouldn't recommend swimming, not with windsurfers about—it can get a bit scary.'

As she paused for breath Siobhan said, 'Actually, I was wondering if I could have a go.'

Zoe looked amazed. 'It's not so easy as it looks, you know,' she said doubtfully. 'It can take a great many lessons, even to—'

'Of course you can,' said Dave softly. 'It's great fun. I can fully recommend it.'

'I know I don't have my own board,' said Siobhan,

'but perhaps I could have the loan of one for a short while or…maybe there are boards for hire?' She glanced back at the clubhouse.

'No need for that,' said Dave. 'There's a spare board in the hut—you can have a go on that. And I'm sure Zoe can fix you up with a wetsuit.'

'You'll still need some tuition,' said Zoe sharply.

'I'll give her all the tuition she needs,' said Dave, and there was a ripple of laughter from some of the others on the beach.

'Watch him, love,' called Josh.

Siobhan looked up and smiled, and as she did so she caught sight of Greg Freeman who was leaning against the side of an upturned rowing boat. He, too, appeared to be watching her, but when he saw she had noticed him he flushed to the roots of his hair.

'Hi, Greg,' she said.

'Oh, hello, Siobhan,' he mumbled, then looked quickly away in embarrassment.

'Come to the clubhouse and we'll get you sorted out,' said Zoe. She spoke quite sharply, and just before Siobhan turned to follow her she caught a glance between two of the other girls.

A little later, wearing a borrowed black wetsuit with shocking pink markings, Siobhan walked to the water's edge, where she found Dave and Josh with the board she was to use. The sail was a bright lime green interspersed with sections of deep blue.

'At least we won't lose sight of you with those colours,' said Josh with a laugh.

'What's your swimming like?' asked Zoe doubtfully, as Dave launched the board.

'I dare say I shall cope,' Siobhan replied lightly.

'Well, let's hope so,' replied Zoe with a sniff, 'because anyone's first time is spent more in the water than on the board.'

For the next five minutes or so Dave gave her instructions—how to stand, how to balance, the basics of sailing, of tacking, of uphauling the rope and manoeuvring the bar that held the sail.

Although she listened, all Siobhan was really aware of was the close proximity of Dave's body in its rubber wetsuit as he stood behind her in the water with his arms around her and his mouth against her ear.

'Now,' he said at last, raising his voice as he backed away from her, 'you're on your own, Siobhan. Give it a try. Take it very easy. I won't be far away.'

Carefully she balanced on the board, her hands uphauling the rope and then gripping the bar. Her eyes narrowed against the glare of the sun on the water, and as the wind caught the sail she turned.

Someone called a warning and she was briefly aware of a sea of faces, watching her from the cove. Then she was away—up and planing the waves with the wind tugging at her hair and whipping tendrils across her face, while salt spray stung her cheeks and the adrenalin coursed through her veins like liquid fire.

For a good ten minutes she flew over the waves, further and further out into the Solent, dipping and turning into the wind then cruising and riding high before at last, reluctantly, turning again and heading for the cove to face the inevitable music.

She skimmed across the shingle to a storm of applause and laughter from the gathered throng. Dave was there to steady her, rueful laughter on his lips and admiration in his eyes as he gripped her hands.

'Why the hell didn't you say?' he murmured.

'I had to make sure I still could,' she gasped, her own

laughter bubbling to the surface. 'Think how silly I would have looked if I'd told everyone I could, only to find I'd forgotten how.'

'Wherever did you learn?' asked Josh, pulling her board further up the beach.

'At home,' Siobhan admitted. 'There's a bay—a bit like this one, actually. I used to go with my brothers and some friends—we also did surfing. The rollers were really huge at times.'

'I feel a right prat,' said Dave, but he was laughing. 'Going on about technique and safety and everything, when all the time...' He placed his arm around her shoulders as they walked up the beach, giving her a quick, brief hug. 'I would say you're easily championship standard.'

'Hardly that,' she protested.

'Go on, admit it,' called Josh. 'You wanted to shock us all.'

'Well, I suppose I did think it would be a bit of fun to see your faces,' Siobhan confessed with a laugh.

'Well, I think it was foolish,' said Zoe primly. 'It could have been dangerous.'

'Don't be daft,' said Josh. 'How could it have been dangerous? It might have been if it had been the other way round—if Siobhan had pretended to know when she didn't have a clue—but this way, well, the laugh was on us for burbling on about tuition and conditions.'

'I was really impressed,' said Greg a little later as they all sat round the tables outside the little café and drank lemonade shandy. 'At first I thought it was just beginner's luck—it took me a few minutes to realise what was really going on.'

'Well, it would, wouldn't it?' snapped Zoe waspishly.

'That's not very nice.' One of the girls, whom

Siobhan had heard the others call Denise, suddenly spoke up. 'Don't you take any notice, Greg,' she added. 'I thought it was a touch of beginner's luck at first as well.' She grinned at Siobhan, then said, 'Hi, there, Siobhan. I'm Denise White, I work on A and E with Helen and this…' she indicated the man at her side '…is my fiancé, Ian.'

Further introductions followed and Siobhan was quickly drawn into the group, which included other staff from the hospital and two of the reception staff from the medical centre. They were a happy, slightly crazy bunch, and in a very short space of time Siobhan knew without a shadow of doubt that she had been accepted and was one of them. It was a good feeling, marred only by Zoe's attitude, which was a shame because Zoe had been the first person to speak to her at the ambulance station, the first one to offer any sort of friendship and the one who had invited her to come to the beach in the first place. The last thing Siobhan wanted was any animosity between them.

As she finished her shandy and Zoe still remained tight-lipped and silent Siobhan resolved that at the first opportunity she would have a word with her, find out what was bugging Zoe and put it right.

The opportunity didn't present itself, however, as Siobhan found herself quickly drawn into the activities and once again was soon skimming across the waves, the only difference being that now she was part of a line of windsurfers. Throughout the rest of the day Dave kept close by her side and they enjoyed the exhilaration of sailing together.

They shared lunch and later, when the offshore breeze dropped, some of the group departed whilst the rest found sandy corners amongst the rocks, stripped down to swimsuits and enjoyed the sun and the water.

Because of her fair complexion Siobhan had to take great care in the sun, smothering herself with a very high-factor sun-cream.

'Let me help with that.'

She looked up to find Dave leaning over her. Taking the tube from her, he squeezed some of the cream into the palm of his hand and when she lay down on her front on her striped beach towel he began applying it to her back with a firm but gentle circular movement. The sensation was so pleasant it was almost erotic and Siobhan closed her eyes, making no protest when he carried on massaging long after she knew the sun-cream would have disappeared into her skin.

Eventually when, with a laugh, he stopped she lazily opened one eye. 'Thanks,' she murmured drowsily.

'My pleasure,' he replied. 'Can't have that lovely Irish skin burning, can we?'

He lay beside her and, very conscious of his presence, his bronzed bare skin and hard body, with the sun on her back, the sound of the sea in her ears and the feel of the sand beneath her, Siobhan allowed herself to drift into that pleasant state that was neither sleeping nor waking, but which hovered dreamily somewhere between the two.

All too soon the day was at an end. The sun was losing its warmth and the breeze increased, whipping up the waves in the Solent into horses with white-crested manes. Others members of the group began gathering their belongings, packing up equipment and preparing to leave.

Siobhan drew on her shorts and shirt over her swimsuit and took a cotton sweater from her beach-bag to drape around her shoulders, loosely knotting the arms before packing her towel and other belongings and beginning the trek back up the slope to the cars.

'I've really enjoyed today,' she said to Dave and Greg, who walked on either side of her. Turning her head, she called over her shoulder to Zoe who was walking behind with Denise, Ian and Josh. 'Thanks for asking me, Zoe.'

Zoe didn't answer and Siobhan bit her lip, wondering yet again what was wrong with her new friend.

When they reached the group of cars there followed a flurry of intense activity as surf boards and sails were secured onto roof-racks and other equipment was stowed away. At last they were all ready to leave, and as Siobhan sat in her Mini Dave drew his car alongside and wound down his window.

'It's been great,' he said. 'You must come again soon.'

'Yes,' she smiled. 'I'd love to.'

There was the usual amusement in his green eyes, together with that look of admiration which she had come to recognise, but this time there was also something else, some other emotion she wasn't quite able to identify.

A hooter sounded behind them and with a glance in his mirror and a muttered exclamation Dave said, 'See you tomorrow.'

This time he didn't call her 'kid', or 'love', or any of the other endearments she had become used to, yet somehow, because there was nothing, it seemed more intimate.

'Yes,' she said faintly, 'see you tomorrow.' She watched as he drove forward, pulling off the grass and away into the lane.

'A word, if you don't mind.'

At the sound of another voice Siobhan turned her head to find that the car that had tooted at Dave was Zoe's, and that she had drawn forward so that now her car was on a level with Siobhan's own. She, too, had her window wound down so there was very little distance between them.

'Oh, Zoe,' said Siobhan, 'of course. In fact, I was wanting to have a word with you. You see, I was rather concerned—'

'Oh? And why was that?' asked the other girl coolly.

'Well, you seemed…I don't know…as if you might be upset about something…as if I might have upset you. I wondered—'

'I'm perfectly all right,' said Zoe in the same cool tones. 'You must be mistaken.'

'Oh,' said Siobhan. 'Oh, I see. Well, that's all right, then.' She frowned, not sure what to say next.

'I heard you say you'd enjoyed yourself,' said Zoe.

'Oh, yes, I have. Very much.' Siobhan paused. 'I'm sorry I tricked you into thinking I'd never done any windsurfing before…'

Zoe shrugged. 'It didn't bother me,' she said, but it clearly had, and Siobhan frowned again, not certain what else she could say. 'I take it you'll be coming again?' Zoe went on when she remained silent.

'Well, yes, I'd love to. I know I'll have to sort something out about equipment—I can't expect to go on borrowing—but—'

'Well, Greg clearly wants you to come again,' said Zoe, turning her head and glancing in her rear-view mirror. 'No doubt he'll help to fix you up with everything you need.' Turning her head again, she gave a false smile.

'Greg?' Siobhan stared at her.

'The guy's obviously smitten with you,' Zoe went on lightly.

'Oh, I don't know about that.' Siobhan gave a short, embarrassed laugh.

'You've only got to see the way he colours up when you're around.' Zoe clearly hadn't finished.

'I think he's a bit like that with any girl,' said Siobhan.

'Well, I would say you're definitely in with a chance there if you play your cards right.' Her tone was firm now, almost dismissive, as if she'd decided on some satisfactory conclusion that required no further discussion.

'Really?' Siobhan laughed. She was far from certain she wanted to be in with a chance. Greg was a dear, and very fanciable, but he was also rather young.

'Yes, I would,' said Zoe. 'Oh, and while we're on that subject, there is just one other thing,' she added lightly.

Siobhan shot her a curious look and saw that two bright spots of colour had appeared on her cheeks. A strange note had also entered Zoe's voice and for one moment Siobhan wondered what on earth she was about to hear.

'Greg's fine. I wish you well with him. Have fun,' Zoe said, with a dismissive little wave of her hand. 'I'm sure he'll be able to provide plenty. But...' she paused, glancing at her nails '...just make sure you stick to Greg, won't you?'

'Whatever do you mean?' Siobhan stared at her across the short distance between the two cars.

'What I say,' said Zoe, pushing the gear lever into first as she spoke. 'Stick to Greg, or anyone else for that matter—just as long as it isn't Dave Morey.' Quite deliberately she allowed her gaze to meet Siobhan's. It was level, almost expressionless, but its meaning was absolutely clear.

'Dave Morey?' said Siobhan faintly.

'Yes,' replied Zoe tightly, 'because he's spoken for.'

'I can assure you,' Siobhan felt her cheeks redden, hating herself for it and wishing it was something she could control, 'I can assure you I have no intention whatsoever of—'

'Good.' Zoe let out her clutch and released her handbrake. 'Because Dave Morey is mine, and I wouldn't want there to be any misunderstanding or confusion.'

With that her car shot forward across the grass and bumped onto the lane, leaving Siobhan to watch her go with a mixture of shock and dismay.

CHAPTER SIX

'HERE we are,' said Dave. 'The Tennyson Memorial School. We're to go to the gym. Apparently, the boy's had an accident on the ropes.'

'I thought it was an asthma attack we were attending,' said Siobhan as she manoeuvred the ambulance through the school grounds.

'It is,' Dave replied shortly. 'It seems the lad had an accident, which in turn brought on an asthma attack. We'll take the nebuliser in with us.'

Groups of children stood around the grounds and the school's main entrance. As Siobhan and Dave, after grabbing a stretcher, ran from the vehicle they could not fail to sense the air of excitement as what would have been just another dull, ordinary Monday suddenly became fraught with drama. They were met on the steps by a rather distracted teacher.

'He's in here,' she gasped. 'He seems in rather a bad way.'

'Does he have medication for his asthma?' asked Dave as they hurried the length of a corridor.

'Yes,' the teacher nodded. 'But, according to Maggie Barlow—she's our nurse—he isn't responding.'

'What about the accident?' asked Siobhan. 'What happened to him?'

'He was at the top of a rope, and for some reason he lost his grip and fell.' As she spoke the teacher flung open the double doors of the gymnasium.

The vast hall was empty save for a little group at the

80

far end—two adults, presumably teachers, an older boy, possibly a prefect, and a young woman in nurse's uniform—all hovering around a boy who was lying on the floor. The nurse looked up as they approached, and when she caught sight of them the relief in her eyes was unmistakable.

'Dave,' she said. Briefly Siobhan found herself wondering if there was anyone who *didn't* know Dave Morey. 'Am I glad to see you. Got a nebuliser with you?'

'Yes.' He turned slightly towards Siobhan who by this time was already on her knees, opening the case of the nebuliser. He crouched down beside the boy. 'Hello, there,' he said. 'What's your name?'

It was obvious the boy didn't have the breath to answer so Dave glanced up at one of the teachers.

'It's William—William Rowe,' said the teacher.

'OK, William, old son,' Dave went on reassuringly, 'we're going to get you fixed up—right away.'

'Do we know his usual medication?' asked Siobhan as she set up the nebuliser.

'Beclomethasone,' said Maggie Barlow, 'and salbutamol if and when he needs it. I've been trying to get him to inhale some, using this...' she held up a plastic volumatic spacer '...but he doesn't seem to be able to draw it in.'

'He'll be better with this.' Siobhan handed the nebuliser mask to the nurse, who placed it in position.

'Any injuries when he fell?' asked Dave, glancing up at the rope that dangled above them.

'He fell very awkwardly.' It was a young man wearing a tracksuit, who looked as if he might be a PE teacher, who answered. 'I think he fell on his shoulder, although I didn't witness the actual incident.'

'He hasn't been moved?' Dave glanced at Maggie, who shook her head. 'Good. Well, when we've got his breathing stabilised we'll get him into a neck brace— just to be on the safe side. Was he complaining of pain after the fall?'

The PE teacher nodded. 'Yes, I would say he was in severe pain, but that was very quickly followed by the asthma attack.'

At that moment there was a commotion as the doors were flung open again.

'It's Mr and Mrs Rowe,' murmured the teacher who had shown Siobhan and Dave into the gym. 'William's parents.'

'Oh, great,' muttered Dave under his breath. 'They might have waited until we got him into the ambulance.'

'Your parents are here, William,' said Maggie Barlow, with a disapproving look at Dave.

'I'll get a brace.' Siobhan scrambled to her feet, and as Mrs Rowe began to have hysterics on catching sight of her son, she hurried thankfully outside to the ambulance.

Because it was morning break there were groups of children everywhere in spite of the efforts of the staff to disperse them.

'Are you a paramedic?' asked one girl as Siobhan opened the back of the ambulance and climbed inside.

'Of course she isn't,' said a boy. 'Only men are paramedics.'

'Then why does it say "Paramedic" on the back of her jacket?' retorted the girl.

'It probably isn't her jacket,' said the boy. 'I bet it belongs to the other one—doesn't it, miss? That jacket—it isn't yours, is it?'

'Actually,' called Siobhan from inside the ambulance, 'it *is* mine.'

'So are you a paramedic?' The boy sounded incredulous.

'Yes,' she replied patiently. 'I'm a paramedic.'

'See! Told you so,' said the girl.

'Is William dead?' called another boy.

'No,' replied Siobhan. 'Of course he isn't dead.'

'He didn't half go with a bang,' said the boy. 'I wondered what had happened.'

'He gets asthma, doesn't he, miss?' called a girl as Siobhan, carrying the neck brace, jumped from the back of the ambulance. 'My sister gets asthma—she can't breathe sometimes. Is that what's happened to William—can't he breathe?'

Carefully avoiding giving any answer that might cause even more speculation among the children, Siobhan secured the ambulance doors. The group watched her in silence, then the boy who had spoken before said curiously, 'What you got there?'

'Don't you know anything?' said the girl disdainfully. 'That's a neck brace, isn't it, miss? I know, I've done a first-aid course with the Red Cross.'

'Yes,' Siobhan agreed as she hurried back up the steps to the sports centre. 'Yes, it is.'

'So, what they want that for?' said someone else.

'To keep his neck in place,' said the first-aid girl importantly.

'Why?'

'In case he's broken it, stupid.'

'Cor, d'you hear that? William Rowe's broken his neck!'

'What?'

'William Rowe—he's fallen off the ropes and broken his neck.'

'Is he dead?'

'Must be. You can't live with a broken neck, dummy.'

Once again, not waiting to hear more, Siobhan fled, but this time back to the relative calm of the gymnasium and William Rowe's hysterical mother.

Together Dave, Siobhan and Maggie Barlow worked steadily. Between them they secured the neck brace, stabilised the boy's breathing, administered a short-acting analgesic for his pain and then, very carefully, transferred him to a stretcher.

'Nice light one this time,' murmured Dave, catching Siobhan's eye as they lifted and carried him from the gymnasium to the waiting ambulance.

By this time the tension and speculation among the steadily gathering crowd of children had reached fever pitch.

'For God's sake, someone, disperse those kids,' rapped out the teacher who had first escorted them into the gym as she caught sight of the crowd.

'It's difficult,' said another, very young teacher, who was standing helplessly on the steps, wringing her hands. 'It's still officially breaktime.'

'Then ring the buzzer—anything,' snapped the first teacher. 'Just get them all inside.'

A brief hush had descended on the crowd, but as Dave and Siobhan gently carried the stretcher down the steps someone shouted the question—the one everyone wanted answered.

'Is he dead?'

As Mrs Rowe gave a strangled cry, it was Dave who answered.

'Dead?' he said, with just the required note of incredulity needed to defuse the situation. 'Of course he isn't dead.' Lifting the boy's mask very briefly, he said, 'You aren't dead, old son, are you?'

Equally briefly, William Rowe raised one hand a few inches off the stretcher and wiggled his fingers.

It wasn't much, but it was enough for his assembled classmates. A faint cheer echoed round the area as Dave and Siobhan secured the boy on one of the couches. Dave looked at Mrs Rowe, who was hovering tearfully at the doors.

'Want to travel with us?' he asked, his tone softer now.

'Oh, yes, yes, please,' she said.

'I'll follow in the car,' said her husband.

As Mrs Rowe climbed aboard Siobhan winked at Dave, before securing the doors, walking round the vehicle and climbing into the driver's seat.

To the accompaniment of the frantic sound of the school buzzer, which was totally ignored by the crowd, and to a further burst of cheering, Siobhan waved, switched on both the siren and the flashing blues and swept out of the school grounds.

'I think I drew the short straw today,' said Dave with a grin as they walked out of A and E a little later. 'I can cope with most things but, I have to admit, neurotic mothers aren't my strong point.'

'You can't blame her,' said Siobhan with a smile. 'She was distraught, poor woman.'

'Yes, I suppose so.' Dave sighed. 'I can understand that. What I couldn't understand was why she kept insisting on talking to William all the way to hospital.'

'Perhaps she was trying to reassure him,' said Siobhan.

'Yes, and that would have been fine if she hadn't ex-

pected him to answer when all the poor lad was trying
to do was clear his airways.'

'I'm glad it was his clavicle and not his neck,' said
Siobhan. 'Actually, I thought that's what it was the minute I saw him.'

'So did I,' agreed Dave, 'but you can't afford to take
any chances.'

They were silent for a while as they drove the short
distance back to the ambulance station. Breaking the silence quite unexpectedly, Dave said, 'Did you enjoy yesterday?'

'Yes,' she said, as she brought the vehicle to a halt
and switched off the engine. 'I did—very much.'

'Well, you certainly fooled us all,' he said. He hesitated for a moment. 'Actually, I sometimes go down to
the cove in the evenings when it's quiet and...I was
wondering, would you care to come with me? We could
go for a sail together—maybe a bit further out this
time—and perhaps, when we get back, go for a drink or
something...'

She was about to say yes, her immediate reaction being that there was nothing she would like better, but
suddenly something stopped her as she recalled Zoe
Grainger's words of the previous day.

Instead, she found herself saying, 'Oh, I don't know
about that, Dave. I think it's probably best if we stick
to weekends and go with the others.'

He didn't answer but she sensed an air of hurt surprise
about him and wished that she hadn't been responsible
for it. They had been getting on so much better in the
last few days and she didn't want anything to change
that again.

Zoe's warning had come as quite a shock. For a start,
Siobhan hadn't realised that there was anything between

Zoe and Dave. Dave had never given the slightest indication that there was anything of that sort, either by
his actions or by anything he said, and Zoe herself had
certainly never as much as even implied it before.

While she had been driving home from the beach
Siobhan had racked her brains to try and recall any word
or gesture that might substantiate the claim, but could
find none. She had come to the uneasy conclusion that
maybe Zoe and Dave had an agreement that while they
were working there should be nothing between them that
could give rise to speculation.

But, then, she'd reasoned, if that were the situation it
would hardly extend itself to their off-duty moments,
and there certainly hadn't been anything during that
whole day on the beach—not an intimate word, a caress
or anything—that could signify a relationship other than
one of casual friendship.

The other aspect, and one which really was more worrying, was why Zoe should have felt the need to warn
Siobhan in the first place. Surely she hadn't given the
other girl reason to believe she was interested in Dave
Morey?

They were colleagues. Nothing more. Nothing less.
The fact that she felt upset that she might have hurt him,
by refusing to go alone to the beach with him, was really
neither here nor there, she thought as Dave got out of
the ambulance and, without waiting for her—indeed,
without even looking back—strode off into the station.

There was a coolness now between them that certainly
hadn't been there before, and it bothered Siobhan. She
found herself watching when Dave and Zoe were in
close proximity to each other, trying to see if there was
more to their relationship than was immediately obvious.

She even found herself wondering if Zoe had gone on holiday with him to Tenerife in those two weeks before she had joined the team.

In the end the possibility bugged her so much that she looked up the holiday rotas and found it there in black and white—Zoe Grainger's annual leave had coincided exactly with Dave Morey's. For Siobhan, that more or less clinched the matter.

Dave and Zoe were quite obviously an item. Why they chose to keep the matter quiet was their business and nothing whatsoever to do with her.

The questions that still niggled at the back of her mind were why, if Dave was so involved with Zoe, he had started paying attention to her, Siobhan, and why, when she had turned him down, he had gone cool on her.

It seemed Helen had been right, after all, when she had warned Siobhan about Dave Morey. Maybe, quite simply, that was it. He was a charmer and a womaniser and Zoe was obviously well aware of it, hence her warning to Siobhan. Maybe it would have made more sense if Zoe's warning had been to Dave—not to her.

But, whatever it was all about, Siobhan made up her mind she wasn't going to lose any sleep over it. She regretted the coolness between herself and Dave, especially as for a while there it had seemed they'd grown close, but there wasn't very much she could do about it.

Towards the end of her second week at the station Siobhan developed a painful throat.

'You must get yourself registered with a doctor,' said Helen, when Siobhan mentioned the fact.

'Who do you suggest?' asked Siobhan.

'Are you used to a male or a female doctor?'

'Well, I'm registered with a lady doctor at home,' she said, 'but—'

'In that case, I suggest Kate Chapman,' said Helen briskly. 'She's first class and very nice into the bargain.'

'Is she the person you were telling me about—the one who's going to marry the locum?' asked Siobhan curiously.

'That's her.' Helen nodded. 'She's a friend of mine. We were at school together.'

'I'll go into the centre on my way to work, get myself registered and see if I can get an appointment,' said Siobhan. 'I've had these throat infections before—I probably need an antibiotic or something.'

She managed to register with Kate Chapman without any problem and to get an appointment for late that afternoon. Her throat grew steadily worse throughout the day, and by the time she and Dave were cleaning the ambulance at the end of their shift she had developed a headache and was feeling quite ill.

Dave had already asked her if she was all right during the course of the day and she had told him, yes, she was fine. Now once again he looked keenly at her.

'Are you sure you're OK?' he said. 'You've been very quiet today.'

'I'm all right,' she said, not wanting to make a fuss. 'Probably just tired, that's all.'

'Good job it's the weekend,' said Dave. He paused. 'You coming to the beach?' It was the first reference he'd made to the beach or windsurfing since he'd asked her to go alone with him and she'd turned him down.

'Yes,' she said lightly. 'I dare say I shall be there.'

He didn't comment at first, just finished what he was doing, but as he jumped from the back of the ambulance he briefly allowed his gaze to meet hers. 'In that case,' he said, 'I dare say I'll see you there—that is, if I go.'

He turned away and walked into the station while Siobhan, by now feeling thoroughly miserable, helplessly watched him go.

'So you're Helen's cousin?' Kate Chapman smiled at Siobhan across the desk. 'Helen told me you were coming to the Island. I understand you're staying in the stable flat?'

'Yes, that's right.' Siobhan nodded.

'My...er...Dr Hammond, our locum, was staying there until...until quite recently.'

'So I believe,' said Siobhan. Unable to help herself, she added, 'I understand from Helen that congratulations are in order.'

Kate smiled again, a radiant smile this time that lit up her face.

There must be something about this being in love lark if it makes you glow like that, thought Siobhan somewhat caustically, feeling, as she did that afternoon, thoroughly wretched.

'Thank you,' said Kate. Glancing down at her notes, she said, 'Now, what can I do for you, Siobhan? As a new patient, I shall want to do a full assessment in due course, but I understand you wanted an emergency appointment today.'

'That's right,' Siobhan replied. 'I'm sorry, I know I should have registered as soon as I arrived but I'm afraid I just didn't get around to it. You know how it is...'

'Of course.' Kate nodded. 'Don't worry about it. Now, what can I do for you?'

'I've developed a very painful throat.'

'Let's have a look.' Kate stood up, picking up a

tongue depressor from a tray. She moved round her desk and turned Siobhan to face the light. 'Right now, open wide,' she said. 'Now, say "ahh". And again. Yes, I see.' Carefully she felt the glands on each side of Siobhan's neck. 'Yes,' she went on, 'these are raised.'

She picked up her auriscope and examined each of Siobhan's ears. 'Yes,' she said at last, 'you do have an infection there. Are you prone to these?'

'Afraid so,' said Siobhan. 'Ever since I was a child.'

'Any other symptoms? Sore chest?'

'No. Although I have a headache and I must admit I do feel a bit shivery.'

'I'll give you a course of antibiotics,' said Kate. 'I suggest you rest for a couple of days. Take paracetamol—that will bring down any temperature—and drink plenty of fluids. Avoid getting any water in your ears. Now, are you allergic to penicillin?'

'No.' Siobhan shook her head.

Briskly Kate entered details into the computer and pressed the print button. While the prescription was printing, without looking at Siobhan, she said, 'Are you on the Pill?'

'No,' Siobhan replied. 'I'm not.'

'That's OK.' Kate nodded. 'I was only asking so as to warn you that the effects of the Pill can be impaired by antibiotics, that's all.' She smiled, tore off the prescription and handed it to Siobhan. 'No relationship at the moment?' she asked.

'No.' Siobhan shook her head, hesitating for a second. 'Even if there was, I wouldn't be on the Pill.'

'Really?' Kate turned to look at her and very slightly raised her eyebrows. 'Is that for ethical or medical reasons?'

'Neither. It's just me...' Siobhan shrugged. 'I...I...

intend saving that for marriage,' she added. She spoke lightly, but with just enough emphasis to show she meant it.

'Well,' said Kate, 'that's quite a refreshing change these days, I must say. The majority of young women I see are really quite sexually experienced by the time that ring goes on their finger.'

'I daresay they are,' said Siobhan.

She went to bed early that night, but slept only fitfully as her throat and ears remained as painful as ever. She felt hot but when she pushed off the bedclothes she felt cold and shivery almost immediately and soon pulled them up around her ears, only for the same thing to happen again and for the same ritual to take place.

It must have been nearly dawn when she finally stopped thrashing around and fell into a heavy sleep.

She was awoken with a start by the sound of a car engine starting up.

Turning over, she peered at her bedside clock. That must be Helen going to work. Damn. That meant she was late. She swallowed. Her throat felt raw. Then she remembered and sank wearily back into her pillows. It was Saturday. Helen may well be on duty that day. She, thank God, wasn't. Even if she had been, she doubted she could have gone in, feeling the way she did. As it was, she was glad she didn't have to take sick leave so soon after starting her job.

She stared at the ceiling. She had been dreaming when the sound of the car had woken her.

What had the dream been about? She had the feeling she had been enjoying it. No, more than that, she'd been enjoying something intensely but, as elusive as most dreams are, the details danced tantalisingly just beyond the reaches of her memory. In the end she was forced to give up.

Her head was throbbing. Gingerly she sat up, swung her legs to the ground and rose carefully to her feet. The room seemed to sway slightly around her and she stood very still for a moment until it righted itself before slowly, she padded into the bathroom.

A little later, while she waited for the kettle to boil, she took her first look out of the window. There was a clear blue sky just visible above the tops of the conifers in the nearby copse. The sun was shining brightly, and even as she watched small fluffy white clouds moved rapidly across the sky.

Perfect windsurfing weather.

It was a pity she wouldn't be down there with them this weekend in the cove. A pity she felt so ill. But even if she hadn't been feeling so bad she couldn't have gone. 'Avoid getting any water in your ears,' Kate Chapman had said. She hadn't been more specific than that, Siobhan thought as she made herself a mug of tea. Hadn't stated exactly what she shouldn't do, but she was pretty certain that windsurfing would come into that category.

Windsurfing.

She stopped and stared at the steam rising from her mug. That was what her dream had been about. Something had flashed through her mind. Now it had gone again. She frowned, concentrating very hard.

Yes, that was it. She had been standing on a very high cliff-top, looking down at a vast stretch of ocean, and she'd seen them as they'd come into view—a long line of windsurfers, gliding and dipping across the water, their sails like dragonflies as they moved in a huge arc far out into the bay.

Someone had been there with her. Standing very close behind her, his body pressed against her own. And that someone had been Dave Morey.

Quite suddenly, but with a deep sense of certainty, she knew. She had turned her face and his lips had brushed her cheek.

Just for one moment the memory was as real, as intense, as if it had really happened, just as now the throb of excitement deep inside her was only too real. Desperately she tried to remember more. But there was no more.

Had they joined the windsurfers? Had they, too, skimmed across those waves far out into the blue of the ocean? Or had they stayed on the cliff-top, standing there so close together with his body against hers, his mouth next to her cheek. And, if they had, what had happened next?

Suddenly, desperately, she wanted to know—longed to know. But that was impossible. It had merely been a dream, and who knew what might have been in that strange, elusive world of lost dreams?

Picking up her mug, Siobhan made her way back to bed. Dave would probably wonder why she didn't join them at the cove. Would he think she was being petty because of the recent coolness between them since she'd turned him down? She hoped not, but if he did there wasn't much she could do about it.

Slowly she sipped the tea, which felt warm and comforting.

On the other hand, she thought, allowing her thoughts to drift to the cove once more, he might not even notice her absence. No doubt Zoe would be there and would claim his attention. It was a shame about Zoe because if it hadn't been for her, Siobhan thought, she could probably have quite got to like Dave.

Not that Helen would have approved of that, of course, after the pains she had taken to warn her about Dave Morey. Siobhan smiled to herself. What was it Helen had said about him? Frowning, she placed her empty mug on her bedside table, leaned back against her pillows and closed her eyes as she tried to recollect.

She'd said he was attractive and was a charmer. Well, both of those were true—he was. She'd also said he had a reputation with the girls, had broken a few hearts—and Siobhan could imagine that quite easily.

But there had been something else. What had that been? What was the term Helen had used to describe Dave? Siobhan searched her mind and as the mists of sleep began to roll in once more she struggled to hold them back.

Something about a rough diamond. Yes, that was it. A rough diamond. It wasn't a term she was familiar with, but that was how Helen had described him. But, far from warning her off, the image it conjured up somehow only made him seem all the more exciting.

As sleep finally claimed her, Siobhan's last hope was that if she concentrated hard enough maybe she could get back into the dream that had slipped away.

And, if she could do that, maybe this time she would find out what happened next.

CHAPTER SEVEN

SIOBHAN didn't get back into her dream but she did sleep for the best part of the day, and by the time Helen returned from work and called into the flat she was feeling a little better.

'I had no idea you were so poorly,' said Helen. 'You should have said last night when you came home. Did you see Kate?'

'Yes.' Siobhan nodded. 'She gave me antibiotics.'

'It's more than a cold, then?'

'Oh, yes. I get these ear and throat infections from time to time,' Siobhan replied. 'Don't worry, they usually clear up with antibiotics in a day or two. I saw a specialist about them once and he was all for taking my tonsils out, but my own doctor at home was against that. He feels these infections will get fewer and fewer as time goes on.'

'Well, is there anything I can get you?' Helen still looked anxious.

'Not really. I have some ice cream in the freezer—that should slide down nice and easily.'

Helen took herself back to The Coach House but a little later she was back with a bowl of her home-made watercress soup, a dish of lemon mousse and a couple of glossy magazines.

'You're spoiling me,' protested Siobhan.

'Only standing in for your mum,' said Helen, drawing back the curtains in the bedroom and opening the window a little. 'I'm sure she would have done the same.'

'It's a good job it's the weekend,' said Siobhan weakly. 'At least it gives me a chance to get over it without having to take any time off.'

'You won't be going in on Monday if you aren't any better,' said Helen firmly.

'You really do sound like my mum now,' said Siobhan.

'Yes, well.' Helen laughed. 'I feel responsible for you.' She glanced round the bedroom, her eyes coming to rest on Siobhan's swimming costume which was hanging on the edge of the radiator. 'Shame you haven't been able to go to the beach,' she said. 'You enjoyed that last weekend, didn't you?'

'Yes, I did,' Siobhan admitted. 'But there will be other weekends.'

'Did you have a go at windsurfing?' asked Helen curiously.

Siobhan nodded.

'Did you enjoy it? I must say it looks very precarious to me. Whenever I've watched anyone they seem to spend more time in the water than on the board.'

'Actually, I've done it before,' Siobhan admitted. 'The boys and I go to a beach near home.'

'Really?' Helen's eyes widened. 'What did the others have to say about that? Were they surprised?'

'You could say that.' Siobhan managed a smile. 'They were prepared to teach me, to show me how. I must confess I led them on a bit, pretending I didn't have a clue. Then, when they got me onto a board, I simply sailed away on my own.'

'I'd love to have seen their faces—I bet they were a real picture.' Helen laughed. 'From what I've heard that little lot think they're the bees knees when it comes to windsurfing.'

'Actually, some of them are very good,' said Siobhan, as she took a spoonful of the lemon mousse and let it slide soothingly down her throat. 'Especially Dave Morey and Greg Freeman.'

'I can quite imagine young Greg Freeman,' said Helen. 'He's built like a Greek god...' She stood up. 'Well, this won't do. I must get on. I've got Richard coming to dinner tonight—he's on call tomorrow so I shall be going in to see Dad, but I'll call in to see you first just to make sure you are all right.'

'Thanks, Helen,' said Siobhan. 'You are very good, you know. You seem to spend your entire life rushing around after other people.'

By the following morning Siobhan was feeling very much better.

'The antibiotics are doing their stuff,' she said when Helen called in briefly, as she had promised, to check on her.

'Good. Well, take things quietly today. I'm going off to see Dad soon. I'll call in again later to see you.'

Siobhan heard the sound of Helen's car as it went down the drive and turned into the lane, heard Chester bark a couple of times to establish his authority and then all was quiet save for the sound of the birds in the tall trees around The Coach House.

She lay for a while in bed, imagining the others as they arrived at the beach for another day's windsurfing, swimming and sunbathing. Suddenly she would have given anything to be joining them, instead of lying there feeling sorry for herself.

Dave would be there. She could picture him getting out of his car, taking his board and sail from the roof-rack and changing into his wetsuit.

Would he even notice that she wasn't there? Probably

not. After all, Zoe would be there and would doubtless occupy his attention. Very soon they would be skimming away together across the bay.

Unable to bear these images any longer, Siobhan miserably got out of bed and took herself to the bathroom, where she showered and washed her hair, before dressing in leggings and a cotton T-shirt.

She had just put the kettle on to make herself some coffee and was wondering if she would take it outside into the sunshine to allow her hair to dry when once again she heard the sound of a car on the drive.

That must be Helen back already, she thought as Chester barked from the house. Maybe Uncle Harry was so unwell today he didn't want anyone to stay for long.

As the kettle came to the boil there came a knock behind her on the outer door of the stable flat.

Siobhan frowned. Helen usually tapped and came in. Turning, she crossed the tiny kitchen and tugged open the door, fully expecting to see Helen at the top of the iron staircase that ran up the outside of the building.

But it was Dave Morey who turned and smiled at her.

'Hello,' he said.

She stared at him in astonishment.

'Oh,' she said at last. 'It's you.'

'Yes,' he said. 'It's me. Were you expecting someone else?'

'I thought…I thought you were Helen. She's been to…to visit her father…' She continued to stare stupidly at him, wondering what on earth he was doing there. He was dressed in jeans and a striped collarless shirt, open at the neck. His short hair looked damp as if he, too, had come straight from the shower…or from the sea.

'Aren't you going to ask me in?' A smile hovered

around his lips and amusement lurked in the green eyes as he saw her obvious surprise.

'Oh, yes,' she said. 'Yes, of course.'

'Nice little place you've got here.' He stepped into the kitchen and closed the door behind him. 'I went to the house first but there wasn't anyone there except for the dog. Then I remembered something about you being in the stable flat. I saw the staircase and put two and two together.'

'But why are you here?' As she stared at him she was aware that her heart, which had leapt painfully at the first sight of him, was now beating fast, very fast indeed.

'I was worried about you,' he said bluntly. 'I thought perhaps you were ill.' He looked closely at her as he spoke then, before she had chance to reply, added, 'Are you ill?'

'Well, yes, as a matter of fact I'm not too good at the moment—'

'I knew it,' he said softly. 'Something told me. I wondered yesterday when you didn't come to the beach, but today, when still you didn't come, I thought there must be something wrong.'

'So you came to find out...?' she said, faintly amazed that he should leave the beach during his precious time off.

'Of course,' he replied, looking steadily into her eyes. 'Like I said, I was worried. I asked some of the others, but none of them seemed to know anything.' He paused, then frowned and said, 'So, what is it, what's wrong?'

'I've got an ear and throat infection,' she said, quickly adding, 'Don't worry, I'm prone to them. I don't think I'm infectious.'

'That doesn't worry me in the slightest,' he said. 'Have you got something for it?'

LAURA MACDONALD

101

'Yes.' She nodded. 'Yes, thanks. I saw Dr Chapman on Friday after work and Helen's been spoiling me rotten.'

'Well, I'm glad to hear it.'

They stood for a moment, looking at each other. Suddenly aware of her wet hair, the fact that she hadn't a scrap of make-up on, and that she was wearing her oldest T-shirt and leggings, Siobhan became flustered but at the same time remembered her manners.

'Would you like some coffee?' she asked, thinking it the least she could do after he had come all the way from the beach to check that she was all right.

'I thought you were never going to ask.' He grinned.

Turning, Siobhan took a second mug from the cupboard above the worktop. Suddenly she didn't know quite what else to say.

In the end, with the two mugs on a tray, together with a plate of digestive biscuits, she said, 'I was about to take my coffee outside to get a bit of fresh air—is that OK with you?'

'Good idea,' he said. 'The sun will dry your hair at the same time.'

She smiled faintly as he opened the door and took the tray out of her hands. 'Give me that,' he said, standing back for her to precede him down the stairs.

She waited for him in the yard. 'Where to?' he asked.

'There's a seat over there outside Helen's back door,' she said.

'Will she mind?'

'I shouldn't think so, especially as she isn't in.' Even as she spoke Siobhan found herself wondering just what Helen would say if she knew Dave Morey was there.

He put the tray on a small rustic table and sat down,

leaning back in the seat, crossing his legs and making himself comfortable.

'I think I'll just let Chester out,' said Siobhan. 'He can hear us and it'll drive him frantic if he can't get out.'

Taking the key from its hiding place beneath one of the many flowerpots, she opened the back door. The red setter rushed out and greeted them both ecstatically, rushing around in circles with his tail wagging furiously.

'He's a lovely dog,' said Dave, taking the mug that Siobhan handed to him.

'Yes, Chester is very special,' she agreed. 'I can remember when he was a puppy, but I'm afraid he's getting old now.'

'How old, exactly?' Dave took a mouthful of his coffee, before setting the mug back on the table.

She frowned. 'Well, now, let's see… I was about ten when they first had him so he must be eleven now—by our years, that is, not doggy ones.'

'So that makes you, what—twenty-one?' He was watching her keenly again.

She nodded and was silent for a while, reflecting, before she said, 'They gave me a big party at home for my twenty-first. I know it's supposed to be at eighteen these days when all that happens, but where I come from old traditions tend to linger.'

Leaning down, Dave began to fondle the deep chestnut of Chester's silky ears. 'So, who are they?' he asked quietly a moment later.

Siobhan frowned, not understanding. 'What do you mean?' she asked.

'You said, *they* gave you a big party. I just wondered who you meant.'

'Oh, my parents…and my brothers…and…and my friends…'

'Ah, he said softly. 'Your friends, the friends you once told me were special.'

'Yes, that's right,' she said, surprised that he should even remember what she had said. 'Yes, I have a lot of friends and…they are pretty special.'

'Maybe there is one who is a bit more special than the others,' he went on after a moment.

'No,' she said quickly. 'No, I don't think so. I would say they are all pretty special…' Suddenly catching his meaning, she flushed slightly. 'Oh,' she said, 'I see what you mean—'

'And?' he said softly. 'I take it there is someone particularly special?'

'I don't know why you should think that,' she said.

'Two reasons.' He sipped his coffee again, watching her in amusement over the rim of the mug. 'It could be the explanation of why you turned me down when I asked you to come out with me, and, secondly, I find it hard to believe that a girl like you doesn't have a steady boyfriend…'

'I'm not saying there haven't been boyfriends,' she said quickly, 'or that there aren't still…but, no, there's no one in particular.'

'So, if that wasn't the reason, could it be that it's me?'

'You?' Her eyes met his.

'Yes, that you find me so repulsive, so repellent, that you simply couldn't stand the thought of my company for even a moment more than is strictly necessary?'

'No, Dave, no.' She was laughing now.

'So what, then?'

'Well…' She paused, hesitating, wondering if she should mention Zoe and the warning that the other girl had given her. Even as she deliberated there came the sound of a car in the drive. They both looked up and Chester's tail began wagging again as Helen's car came into view.

When she remained silent Dave sighed and said, 'It's my reputation, isn't it?'

'What do you mean?' she protested, laughing, as out of the corner of her eye she watched Helen park her car and get out.

'You've been told all sorts of lurid stories about my love life—haven't you? Go on, admit it.' He, too, was laughing now as Helen walked towards them.

'Maybe I have,' Siobhan replied lightly. 'What I don't know is whether or not those stories have any truth in them.'

'If you were to come out with me, maybe you would find out,' he said out of the corner of his mouth.

'Helen.' Siobhan looked up and Dave got to his feet. 'How was Uncle Harry?'

'A little brighter today, I think,' Helen replied. Looking coolly at Dave, she said, 'This is a surprise, Dave, finding you here.'

'He was worried about me,' said Siobhan quickly, 'because I wasn't at the beach. Wasn't that kind of him, Helen, to come and find out what was wrong?'

As Dave drained his mug Helen was forced to agree as, with Chester at her side, she made her way into the house.

He pulled a face. 'I don't think Helen approves of me,' he said. 'I guess she thinks I'll lead you astray.'

'There's no fear of that,' Siobhan replied. 'I'm more than able to take care of myself.'

Dave smiled. 'You know something?' he said, looking into her eyes again. 'I would be inclined to agree with that. Anyway, I'd best be off now. You take care and, don't forget, if you're not right tomorrow, promise me you'll take some time off.'

'Yes, all right, I promise.' She stood up. 'Oh, and Dave?'

He had turned to go but he paused and looked back at her. 'Yes?'

'Thank you for coming to see me. I do appreciate it.'

He gave her his quick, infectious grin and was gone. His car—a battered Escort—pulled away down the drive with a noisy toot of the horn.

The dust had barely settled in his wake when Helen came back into the yard. 'So, what did he really want?' she said, a touch of sarcasm in her voice.

'I told you,' Siobhan protested. 'He was concerned, that's all. Honestly,' she added with a laugh when she saw Helen's sceptical look. 'It was the concern of one colleague for another. He knows I'm new here and that I don't know many people. He guessed I wasn't well when I didn't turn up at the beach for the second day running, and, let's face it, he wasn't to know how you would spoil me, was he?'

'Huh!' Helen began dead-heading the geraniums in the box outside the kitchen window.

'You don't believe that for one moment, do you?' said Siobhan.

'How did you guess?' said Helen.

'Why don't you like him?' Siobhan asked curiously.

'I didn't say I didn't like him,' Helen replied. 'As it happens, believe it or not, I do. He's good-hearted and he makes me laugh.'

'Then why…? I don't understand…'

'I told you, Siobhan, it's the devastation he seems to cause among the female community. I've lost count of the number of my nurses he has dated since he's been with the paramedics. It usually ends in disaster and it's the likes of me who are left to pick up the pieces.'

'Why do these affairs end in disaster?' said Siobhan after a while.

'Generally, because the girls take him seriously, but for Dave Morey it's all just a bit of fun.'

'Well, you certainly need have no such fears on my behalf,' said Siobhan firmly.

'You mean to tell me he hasn't asked you out?' Helen turned from the window-box, the red petals clasped in her hand.

Siobhan didn't answer, bending instead to pat Chester who was nuzzling around her legs.

'He has. Hasn't he?' Helen demanded accusingly.

'Well…well, now you come to mention it…'

'I knew it!' said Helen. 'I knew he would try to chat you up the first opportunity he got.'

'You needn't worry.' Siobhan laughed. 'I turned him down.'

'Oh, and why was that? I find it hard to believe it was anything to do with my warning.' Helen raised one eyebrow.

'Actually, it was more to do with something that Zoe Grainger said,' Siobhan replied.

'Zoe Grainger?' Helen frowned. 'What's she got to do with anything?'

'Well, she issued a warning as well, but it was a little different from yours, Helen. I rather got the impression that she and Dave are an item at the moment and that she didn't want any competition.'

Helen turned and stared at her. 'Are you sure?' she said quietly.

Siobhan nodded. 'Quite sure.'

'Well, if that's the case,' said Helen, briskly rolling the geranium petals into a ball, 'it illustrates even more why Dave Morey is not someone you'd want to get involved with.'

'Oh?' Siobhan frowned. 'And why is that?'

'I don't know whether or not you are aware of the fact...' Helen tossed the ball of petals into a nearby wastebin '...but Zoe Grainger just happens to be married.'

Siobhan stared at Helen. It was the last thing she had expected to hear.

'Well,' she said, 'I can assure you, she certainly warned me off. But now you tell me this, it answers something that I couldn't quite understand.'

'And what is that?'

'If Zoe and Dave are having an affair, they are certainly keeping the whole thing very quiet. There hasn't been the slightest indication that there is anything between them, either at work or when I saw them at the beach.'

'Well, that's why,' Helen replied crisply. 'I can't imagine Dave would be too keen for Mal Grainger to find out. I can't imagine Ted Carter being too pleased either. From what I've heard, he doesn't take too kindly to that sort of thing among members of his staff.'

'You mean, Zoe's husband works for Ted as well?' Siobhan looked startled. She certainly hadn't heard of a Mal Grainger on the staff, but that didn't mean to say there wasn't one. He might not be a paramedic. There were others she hadn't met yet—ancillary staff, or those in the control room.

But Helen was shaking her head. 'No,' she said, 'he's Fire Service—but it's close enough. And, I can assure you, Ted Carter wouldn't approve.'

Siobhan sank onto the garden seat again. Suddenly she felt quite weak.

'You're still looking peaky, you know, Siobhan,' said Helen, looking at her. 'I think you should get yourself back upstairs and have some more rest.'

'Yes, I think you might be right,' said Siobhan. Suddenly she felt as if all the fight had gone out of her. Her head was aching again and her legs felt decidedly shaky. Without any further word of protest she made her way back to the flat.

The following morning Helen put her foot down and said there was no way she was letting her go in to work and Siobhan didn't have the energy to argue.

Much later, during the afternoon, the local florist delivered a dozen red roses with a little card attached that said, 'With Love from Dave.' She was more than glad that Helen was well out of the way. She didn't feel strong enough to face her cousin's wrath and indignation at what Siobhan knew Helen would call the audacity of a man who could send red roses to one woman while engaged in a clandestine affair with another, who just happened to be married.

CHAPTER EIGHT

'IT'S a call from the police.' Dave switched on the blues. 'An incident in the shopping precinct. Good grief,' he added, 'will you take a look at this traffic? Come on, move, you lot.' As the siren began to wail some motorists began to move over, although others continued to crawl along, totally oblivious to any sense of drama or urgency.

Siobhan cast a sidelong glance at Dave as he began to weave their vehicle through the morning shoppers and holiday-makers. His face was set with determination but as the way ahead suddenly cleared and he was able to put his foot down he must have sensed her looking at him for he threw her a quick glance and winked at her.

Her heart gave a funny little leap and suddenly she found herself wishing that Zoe Grainger didn't work at the station, that she was content with her husband and that there wasn't anything going on between Zoe and Dave.

It was strange when she thought about it because she hadn't been too bothered about him to start with. She'd been intrigued certainly, especially after Helen's warning, attracted even when they'd first met, but not much more.

It had only been since she'd got to know him better that she'd gradually come to realise just how much she liked him, only to find that he was involved elsewhere. Life could be unkind at times.

She had returned to the station that morning after being forced to take two days' sick leave. It had been exceptionally busy and she'd had no time to speak to Dave or even to thank him for the flowers.

The call to the precinct had immediately followed the previous call, which had been to take a woman with a threatened miscarriage to the obstetric unit at the Shalbrooke.

'Did they say what this was about?' asked Siobhan, as Dave swung the ambulance into the precinct.

'Not really,' Dave replied. 'They simply said an incident.'

There was the usual crowd of onlookers, held in check by several uniformed police officers. One of the officers approached Dave and Siobhan as they jumped down from the ambulance.

'A fight,' he said. 'We've taken most of them into custody, but two are pretty badly injured with stab wounds.' He led the way to a shop entrance where one figure was lying on the ground, half propped up against the glass shop front. He was a youngish man with a mass of dreadlocks, and wearing a huge overcoat in spite of the heat of the summer's day. He was muttering to himself and trying to push away a policeman who was desperately attempting to help him.

'Thank God, you're here,' said the policeman as he caught sight of Dave and Siobhan. 'This one just doesn't want to be helped.'

'Who else is there?' Dave looked round.

The policeman nodded towards the doorway of a shoe shop. 'There's another one over there.'

'Right, Siobhan,' said Dave, 'you take that one. I'll see to our friend here.'

Siobhan hurried across the large paved area. This patient was being attended by a WPC, and there seemed to be a great deal more blood.

'He's in a bad way,' said the policewoman, looking up at Siobhan.

Siobhan sank to her knees, unlatched her case and, mindful of the last occasion, pulled on a pair of surgical gloves.

'What the hell's with you?' gasped the man on the ground, lifting his head to watch her. 'You think I've got AIDS or summat?'

'No,' replied Siobhan coolly, her gaze meeting his. 'But can you be sure that I haven't?'

The man sank back onto the pavement and was silent after that, making no protest as Siobhan checked for stab wounds. There was one slash down his cheek and onto his neck. This wound was bleeding profusely. There was a second stab wound just below his left shoulder, this cut looked as if the knife had penetrated deeply while a third was somewhere in the region of the ribs on his left side. He was wearing a denim jacket and jeans, which were slowly turning a deep purple as the blood soaked the indigo material. His head was shaven, there were large gold hoops in each ear and he had a skull tattooed on his right cheek.

Quickly Siobhan took pads from her case and covered the wound sites. 'Could you hold these in place to stem the bleeding?' she said to the WPC.

She checked the man's blood pressure, which she found to be low. 'I need to set up a drip to replace lost fluids,' she explained, taking a bag of Haemaccel from her case together with a cannula.

Within minutes the life-saving fluid was dripping into a vein in the man's hand, while Siobhan set about securing the pads firmly in place.

'Everything all right here?' She glanced up to find Dave, standing above her.

'Yes, fine,' she said. 'He's lost a lot of blood, but he'll do. What about the other one?' She glanced across the precinct.

'Yes, he'll make it, too,' said Dave. 'He's as high as a kite. I doubt he even knows what's happened.'

'Is that what this was all about?' said Siobhan, getting to her feet and looking at one of the policemen.

'Oh, undoubtedly,' the officer replied. 'One of them is a pusher, but we're not sure which one yet.'

'They both need further treatment,' said Dave. 'We'll have to transport them to A and E at the Shalbrooke,' he said to the police officer.

'In that case, you'll need an escort,' the officer replied.

'That probably would be a good idea.' Dave nodded.

Both men were transported to the ambulance, where one of the male police officers climbed aboard.

Siobhan was watching Dave and wondering what he would do next. She saw him pause and then, catching her eye, he said, 'I don't suppose it's any good my offering to attend?'

'Not a bit of good,' she said cheerfully. 'You're driver today.'

'OK.' He shrugged and was about to jump out of the back of the ambulance when he stopped and caught her arm. 'Are you sure?' he said, his gaze meeting hers.

'Of course, I am,' she said. Seeing the real concern in his eyes, she added, 'Dave, I'll be fine. I'll have the officer with me, and I don't think either of these two are going anywhere. One's completely spaced out and they are both so weak from loss of blood...'

'All right.' Dave nodded, jumped to the ground and fastened the doors.

This time Siobhan felt no indignation at his inference that it might be better if she weren't involved. This time she just felt touched at his obvious concern.

'I wouldn't have thought drugs were too much of a problem here,' Siobhan said to the police officer as Dave started the ambulance and, with siren sounding and flashing blues, they swept out of the precinct and headed for the Shalbrooke.

'I guess it's a problem everywhere these days,' the officer replied. 'I suppose it's inevitable wherever there is coastal access.'

Siobhan kept a close watch on both patients during the drive, but they reached A and E without further incident. She and Dave, together with the police officer, transferred the two men into the treatment room and the care of the casualty staff.

They were on their way out when Helen called out to them from behind the reception desk. 'Hello, you two. How are you feeling, Siobhan?'

'I'm fine, thanks, Helen,' she replied.

'That's good,' Helen replied. 'Don't go overdoing it on your first day back to work.' She was about to turn away when she stopped, as if she'd suddenly remembered something. 'Oh, Dave?' she called. When he looked back she went on, 'We've been wondering about the disco for the Summer Barbeque. Are you able to help us out again?'

'I'm afraid there's a problem,' said Dave ruefully. 'I'm on duty that weekend. I won't be finished until about nine o'clock that night.'

Siobhan threw Dave a swift glance. If he was on duty that night it meant she was as well, which was a shame because she had been looking forward to the hospital's Summer Barbeque.

'Oh, that's a pity,' said Helen. She paused then said, 'What about Pete? Do you think he would still be prepared to do it?'

Dave hesitated. 'I wouldn't have thought so,' he said. 'I'm afraid Pete isn't doing very much at all these days. But leave it with me for the time being. I'll try and come up with something.'

'I've been thinking,' said Siobhan a little later as they were cleaning the ambulance after finishing their shift. 'Don't you think that might be just the thing for Pete?'

'How do you mean?' asked Dave.

'Well, I wouldn't have thought it would involve anything that was physically beyond his capabilities. It sounds as if it was something that you both enjoyed doing—and didn't you say you donated the proceeds to charity?'

Dave nodded. 'Yes,' he said slowly. 'It all went to research into kidney disease.' He paused. 'And you're right,' he went on after a moment, 'we did enjoy it. I've been hoping we could continue with it but, like I said, when I mentioned it to Pete he quite simply didn't want to know.'

'When was that?'

'A couple of months ago—something like that.'

'Around the time of Pete's diagnosis?'

'Well, yes, now you come to mention it, I suppose it was,' he replied. 'I thought at the time it might cheer him up a bit, but I was obviously wrong. He wasn't having any of it.'

'It was too soon, Dave,' Siobhan said gently. 'The poor man had just been dealt a body blow. He probably couldn't even think straight, let alone put his mind to anything else.'

'Yes, I guess so…' Dave ran one hand over his short hair in a helpless sort of gesture.

'I think now, though,' Siobhan went on, 'you might find it's a different story. He's had time to come to terms with his condition and, who knows, he just might be sitting there, wanting to do something but not knowing quite how to start. He may even be thinking that you might have gone off the idea as you haven't mentioned it again.'

'I didn't like to…' Dave shook his head. 'He seemed so depressed.'

'Sometimes it's the best way—not to keep pussyfooting around but to act perfectly naturally and help someone to face up to the truth.'

He turned his head and stared at her. 'You sound as if you know,' he said quietly.

'I told you,' she said. 'I've done quite a bit of voluntary work with the handicapped at home.'

'Oh, yes,' he said, 'the Lourdes trips…' He took a deep breath. 'I think I'll go and see Pete again and ask him about the disco.' He glanced at his watch. 'I wonder, would you come with me?'

'Oh… I don't know about that,' she began, but he cut her short.

'Please,' he said. 'I'd like you to.'

'Are you sure it would be a good idea? Me, I mean. I can't imagine I'm exactly his favourite person, having taken his job.'

'Maybe not. But it's a fact that you have. And you've just said yourself how important it is to face up to facts and to act normally in these situations. Come on, Siobhan, you did say that.'

'Yes,' she admitted. 'Yes, I did…'

'So you'll come, then?' he asked eagerly.

'Oh, all right,' she said at last.

'Good.' He jumped down from the back of the ambulance and, taking her arm, steadied her as she did the same. 'We'll take my car,' he said, 'then I'll bring you back here to collect yours.'

She hesitated fractionally, then silently admonished herself for even thinking that this could simply be a ploy on Dave's part to get her into his car. Helen might think that. Probably would. But how could she think it when they were so obviously engaged on a mission of mercy?

She was, however, overwhelmingly relieved that there was no one else around to witness her getting into Dave's car and driving out of the staff car park with him.

God knew what Zoe Grainger would have made of it. Siobhan was thankful that Zoe was on a late shift and out on a call.

Thinking of Zoe suddenly reminded her of the flowers Dave had sent her—the flowers he shouldn't have sent if he was involved with someone else—and the fact that she hadn't yet thanked him for them.

Taking a deep breath but keeping her gaze on the road ahead, she said, 'Oh, Dave, I've been meaning all day to say thank you...thank you very much for the flowers. It...er...it was very kind of you.'

'It was my pleasure.' Turning his head, he smiled at her.

'Really, you know,' she went on after a short pause, 'you shouldn't have sent them.'

'Why not?' He sounded genuinely surprised.

'Well...' Suddenly she was lost for words. 'Well, you just shouldn't have, that's all.'

'Don't you like roses?'

'Oh, yes, yes, I love roses.'

'But you don't like red roses, is that it?' he persisted.

'What?' She was getting flustered now when all she'd wanted to do was to tell him that the last thing he should be doing was sending her red roses when he had just taken someone else to Tenerife.

'You don't like the colour red?' His tone was serious but an amused smile tugged at the corners of his mouth.

'Yes, of course I do.' She sighed. 'It's just that, well, let's face it, Dave, red roses have always been known to have a certain significance.'

'Really?' He grinned. 'You mean, if a man sends them to a lady?'

'Well, yes…'

'I know,' he said, drawing the car up before Pete Steel's house. He added, 'Well, here we are. Let's see if you can work your charm on Pete and persuade him that it's in his best interests to do the disco.'

'Actually,' said Siobhan coolly as she stepped out of the car and shut the door, 'I do happen to think it is.'

'Yes, quite.' Dave grinned as he led the way up the garden path of the Steels' neat red-bricked semi and rang the doorbell.

The pretty dark-haired woman opened the door. A look of surprised pleasure crossed her features when she saw Dave, then her gaze flickered to Siobhan.

'Hi, Sue,' said Dave. Turning slightly, he said, 'This is Siobhan. We've come for a word with Pete, if that's OK?'

'Course it is, Dave.' Sue hesitated slightly, then nodded to Siobhan, before stepping aside to allow them to squeeze into the narrow hallway. 'You can come any time, you know that,' she added as she closed the front door. 'You're the only person I know, Dave, who has a hope in hell of cheering him up.'

'That bad, eh?' Dave raised his eyebrows.

'Worse,' Sue replied, pulling a face.

'So, where is he?'

'Where he always is,' she replied. 'Sitting in his chair, either in front of the telly or in front of the window.' Stepping over children's toys, she led the way into the sitting room.

As she had predicted, Pete was in front of the television. There was a quiz show on. He looked up as they entered but made no attempt to switch off the programme, even though he had the remote control clutched in one hand.

'Pete, my old son, how are you?'

Siobhan detected a trace of forced gaiety in Dave's tone.

'I've brought someone for you to meet,' he went on, when Pete remained silent. 'This is Siobhan O'Mara. Siobhan...' he briefly turned to her '...this is Pete Steel, my old sidekick.'

'Hello, Pete.' Siobhan stepped forward and was about to put out her hand but, uncertain how good his coordination was, thought better of it and simply smiled and nodded.

He stared at her for a long moment. His gaze moved over her from top to toe, taking in every detail of her slight figure—from her auburn curls, tamed today into a single plait, her turquoise sweatshirt, white cotton jeans and even to the Italian-style loafers she wore on her bare feet.

'So you're my replacement,' he said tightly at last.

'That's right, and I must say what a hard act yours is to follow.' Oh, God, she thought, her attempt at normality sounded even more strained than Dave's.

An awkward silence followed until Sue said, 'I'll go

and make some tea.' She seemed glad to escape to the kitchen. Siobhan wished she could go with her, and was just wondering whether she quite dared to offer to help when Dave spoke.

'Siobhan is Helen Turner's cousin,' he said. 'She's come over from Ireland and is living at the stable flat at Helen's house.'

During the next silence Siobhan found herself desperately searching for something to say.

'What part of Ireland do you come from?' asked Pete suddenly, unexpectedly.

'County Cork,' Siobhan replied, ridiculously pleased that he should be interested. 'Do you know it?' she added, not for one moment imagining that he would.

'Yes.' He nodded. 'We go there.' He paused and, correcting himself, said. 'Or rather we used to go there on holiday sometimes…' His gaze moved to the large picture window at the far end of the room.

Two small boys were playing in the garden, and just for the moment Siobhan could well picture the family holidays in Ireland, with swimming and other open-air sporting activities. The sort of holidays that for Pete were a thing of the past.

She was just wondering what else she could say that wouldn't evoke too many painful memories when Pete looked round at Dave and said, 'Talking of holidays, how did yours go? I forgot to ask you last time you came in.'

Siobhan felt herself stiffen. Suddenly, the last thing she wanted was to hear about Dave's holiday in Tenerife.

'It was brilliant,' he said, confirming her worst fears that he most likely had been with Zoe. 'You know, plenty of sea, sun and sangria.'

Siobhan swallowed. For one awful moment she'd thought he'd been going to say sea, sun and sex, which realistically, when she thought about it, was probably exactly what it had been.

'Was Joe all right?' asked Pete.

Dave nodded. 'Yes, he was fine. He's been on dialysis a couple of times since he got home. But he was fine out there.'

Siobhan frowned. Who was Joe?

At that moment Sue returned with the tea. She had obviously heard the last remarks for, as she set the tray down, she asked, 'Did Christine enjoy herself?'

'Oh, yes.' Dave grinned. 'She had a wonderful time. It did her good. Life's been pretty tough since Terry left her. Sandy enjoyed it as well. I can't believe how those kids are growing up. Speaking of which, Pete, the social club is in a bit of a spot and I was wondering if you could help out.'

Immediately Pete looked wary. 'What do you mean?'

'They don't have a DJ for the disco at the Summer Barbeque.'

'I thought you'd be doing it.' Pete scowled.

'I would normally,' said Dave, 'but as it happens Siobhan and I are on a late that night.'

'Can't you swap shifts with anyone?' said Pete.

'You're joking,' said Dave with a laugh. 'On a Saturday night? And the night of the barbeque? Come on, Pete, you know no one would swap that... No, it's a bit of a problem.'

'So what do you want me to do about it?' asked Pete. Siobhan noticed he avoided Dave's gaze.

'I was hoping you might be able to do it,' said Dave. He said it casually but Siobhan noticed a little throb of tension in his voice. She couldn't help but think that if she, who had known him for such a short length of time, had recognised it then surely Pete, who had worked with him for so long, would be aware of it.

'I don't know how you can even suggest it,' said Pete. 'What use would I be? I'd probably drop all the discs.'

'I'd help you,' said Sue suddenly. 'You could do all the patter and I could sort out the discs and put them on.'

'There you are,' said Dave eagerly. 'Perfect solution.'

'I don't know…' Pete shook his head.

'I could take over later in the evening if it got too much,' said Dave.

Pete still looked dubious.

'What will they do if neither you nor Pete can do it?' asked Sue as she poured the tea.

'Well, like I say, I think they'll have a problem.' Dave shrugged. 'They've got so used to us doing it that they've left it too late to book anyone else. The mobile ones will all be booked up by now. There are always a lot of mid-summer activities on the Island—fêtes and barbeques,' he added for Siobhan's benefit.

'And there's no one else who would be willing to have a go?' said Sue, passing a cup of tea to Siobhan.

'Nope.' Dave shook his head as he took the cup Sue now handed to him and began to stir his tea. Quite casually, he said, 'Apart from Barry, of course.'

'Barry?' said Pete quickly.

Dave nodded. 'Yes, apparently he's offered. You know he's always fancied himself as a DJ. Couldn't wait to get his hands on the equipment.' He shrugged again. 'Looks like I may have to let him have a go under the circumstances.'

'You mean our Barry?' asked Siobhan curiously. 'Barry Weston?' Somehow she couldn't quite imagine it—the dour Barry Weston was the last person she could see as a disc jockey.

'That's the one.' Dave took a sip of his tea and replaced the cup in the saucer.

'I'll do it,' said Pete, and they all looked at him.

'Will you really, old son?' Dave raised his eyebrows in surprised pleasure. 'Well, that's marvellous. I'm sure you'll manage all right, especially if Sue lends a hand until I can get there. And you can't get away from the fact that it's all in a very good cause.' He turned to Siobhan. 'All proceeds to kidney research—including our fee,' he said.

'All right,' said Pete irritably. 'You've made your point. There's no need to go on about it. I've said I'll do it—OK?'

'Did he really offer? Barry Weston?' Siobhan asked suspiciously a little later when she and Dave were back in his car.

'What?' He gave an abstracted frown as he raised his hand to Sue who stood in the doorway, watching them go.

'Barry Weston,' she repeated a trifle impatiently. 'Did he really offer to do the disco for the Summer Barbeque?'

'Not as far as I know.' Dave shook his head. 'That's not to say he wouldn't have when he found out they were looking for someone. Like I said just now, it's a well-known fact that he couldn't wait to have a go.'

'But,' she spluttered, 'you told Pete—'

'I know.' He grinned. 'And it worked, didn't it? It was a stroke of pure genius. It came to me quite suddenly while we were talking.'

'What do you mean?' Siobhan frowned.

'Pete likes Barry Weston about as much as I do. He

also knows that Barry was jealous when we took over the disco. Our popularity ratings soared, you see, especially with the nurses, and Barry couldn't stand it. And Pete also knows he would give anything to take over.'

'Well, like you say,' said Siobhan with a laugh, 'it worked. Let's hope it'll be the start of something for Pete. There are so many things he'll be able to do once he's over his depression.'

'I know,' Dave agreed. 'But it's all down to motivation, and without that he won't do anything.'

Siobhan was silent for a moment as she looked at him curiously.

'Who's Joe?' she asked.

He turned his head to look at her until with an exclamation he had to swerve the car to avoid a tractor which was attempting to pull out of a field. 'Should look before he pulls out,' he muttered under his breath. 'Joe?' he said.

'Yes,' Siobhan replied. 'I wondered who he was. When you were talking about him it sounded as if he has kidney trouble.'

'Oh, he does,' said Dave. 'He has to go for dialysis. He's had trouble almost from the day he was born. I think it'll end up in him having a transplant. Joe's the reason I became involved in raising funds for kidney research in the first place.'

'Who is he exactly?' Siobhan looked bewildered.

'Joe? Oh, sorry, didn't I say? He's my nephew,' said Dave.

'Your nephew?' Siobhan was amazed. It was the last thing she'd expected to hear.

'Yes, he's my sister Christine's boy.'

'So.' She hesitated slightly. 'Did he go to Tenerife with you?'

'Yes.' Dave nodded. 'It was a bit of a gamble but we had full co-operation between the two hospitals—his local hospital on the mainland, that is, and the one in Tenerife. Luckily, as I said to Pete, we didn't have any problems while we were there. Anyway, they all seemed to enjoy themselves...'

'All?' she said faintly.

'Yes, Christine came as well, and her daughter—my niece—Sandy.' He chuckled. 'Everyone thought we were a family. It was quite an experience for me, I can tell you.'

Siobhan was silent but her mind was working overtime.

'What's up?' he said a moment later. 'You seem puzzled about something.'

'I am, actually,' she replied.

'What about?'

She took a deep breath. 'Did anyone else go to Tenerife with you?'

He frowned. 'No, not as far as I know,' he replied. 'Why? Who else should there have been?'

'Oh, no one.' Suddenly she felt foolish.

'No, go on,' he said curiously. 'What did you mean?'

'It was nothing—just something I assumed, that's all.'

'You can't leave it there.' He laughed. 'I shall die of curiosity. You'll have to tell me now. Come on,' he urged, 'who else did you think had gone with me?'

'Well, actually,' she said stiffly, feeling even more silly than ever, 'it was Zoe, Zoe Grainger.'

'Zoe Grainger?' He threw her a startled glance, once again taking his eyes from the road. This time the car wandered slightly and he was forced to straighten it. 'Whatever made you think that?'

She hesitated, thinking that whatever she said now she

could end up sounding quite ridiculous. 'Well, it was something that Zoe herself said...' She trailed off but when she threw Dave an uncertain glance she realised that his jaw had tightened.

'I think,' he said, 'I've got a pretty good idea what that might have been.'

'You have?' she said in relief.

He nodded grimly then, glancing at his watch, he said, 'Listen, are you in a hurry to get home?'

'Well, no,' she replied. 'Not especially. Why?'

'In that case,' he said, 'I suggest we go somewhere for a quiet drink. There are a few things I think we need to talk about.'

CHAPTER NINE

AFTER the heat of the sultry June day it was cool in the corner of the old thatched pub, with its oak-beamed ceilings and flagstoned floor. Siobhan watched Dave as he stood at the bar, ordering their drinks. She'd very nearly chickened out at the last moment and demanded he took her back to the station car park, mindful of Helen's dire warnings about having any sort of involvement with this man.

But something had stopped her. She wasn't entirely sure what. Whether it was curiosity over what she might be about to hear, or the effect that his smile seemed to have on her—like it did right now, as he turned from the bar and caught her eye over the tops of the two glasses he was carrying—or whether it was simply because she liked him, and the more she got to know him the greater that liking was becoming.

Carefully he set the glasses down on the table and sat down opposite her on a wheel-backed chair.

'Cheers,' he said, lifting his glass. He took first a sip that left a line of froth on his upper lip and then a long mouthful.

'I needed that.' He sighed and set his glass down. 'It's been quite a day.' He watched her as she raised her own glass and took a sip. 'And I've got the feeling it isn't over yet.'

Siobhan smiled but, not giving her time to answer, Dave leaned back in his chair, rested one leg across his knee and, linking his hands behind his head, said, 'So, what did she say, then?' There was a half-smile on his face as he spoke.

Siobhan remained silent for a moment, considering her answer, but Dave mistook her silence. 'Come on,' he said. 'I want to know.'

'She warned me off,' she said at last.

As his smile slowly disappeared Dave stared at her.

'She told me,' Siobhan went on quietly, 'that I was welcome to Greg Freeman, or to anyone else for that matter, but that—'

'What's Greg Freeman got to do with anything?' Dave interrupted.

'What do you mean?'

'Well, why should Zoe have said that?'

'I don't really know...' She shrugged helplessly. 'I expect—'

'Had you said you fancied him?'

'No, not exactly.' She took a deep breath. 'I might have said I thought he was very nice and that he seemed to blush whenever he saw me, but I've since realised that poor Greg seems to blush when he talks to any girl...'

'OK.' He grinned. 'Go on.'

Siobhan got the impression he was enjoying himself. 'Where was I?' she said. He'd flustered her, talking about Greg, and she was faintly annoyed with herself.

'You were saying that Zoe had told you you were welcome to Greg Freeman or to anyone else,' he said calmly.

'Oh, yes, that's right,' she said. 'But then she said that you were spoken for,' she continued. 'That you were hers.'

Slowly Dave lowered his arms. 'When did she say this?' he said quietly.

'That Sunday when we were all at the beach. It was just as we were leaving. You drove away first, then Zoe drew her car alongside mine, wound down her window and—well, that's what she said.'

'So what did you think?' He narrowed his eyes.

Siobhan shrugged. 'What was I to think? I was surprised, I have to admit that.'

'Why were you surprised. Because Zoe's married?'

'I didn't even know that at the time,' she protested. 'No, I was surprised for other reasons. Mainly, I suppose, because I hadn't detected any sign between you and Zoe that you were having any sort of relationship. Later, after I found out that she was married, I put that down to the fact that you had to be discreet at work in case rumours got back to Ted, whom I gather is very anti that sort of thing...' She shrugged again, trailed off and took another sip of her drink.

Dave leaned forward watching her closely. 'And?' he said at last.

'And what?'

'You said there were reasons—that was only one. What was the other—or others?'

'Well...' She hesitated. Allowing her gaze to meet his fully, she said, 'You had rather been trying to chat me up...and I thought...well... Oh, it doesn't matter what I thought.' She waved her hand in a dismissive little gesture.

'Yes, it does,' he said quickly. 'It does matter—it matters very much.'

When she remained silent he went on, 'So, let's get this straight. Here was you, thinking I was interested in you, then you get a warning from another woman to lay off because this other woman and myself supposedly have some heavy relationship going. Is that right?'

'Something like that, yes,' she mumbled, picking up her glass and burying her nose in it again. She was beginning to wish she hadn't started this, to wish she'd gone home when she'd had the chance. Suddenly, the sanctuary of the stable flat seemed very appealing.

'What led you to believe that Zoe had been on holiday with me?' Dave was speaking again and she forced her mind back to what he was saying, willing herself to concentrate. 'Did she tell you that?' he added, and there was a definite note of suspicion in his voice now.

'Oh, no. No,' said Siobhan hastily setting her glass down again. 'No, she didn't say that...'

'So how...? Why...should you even think it?' He looked puzzled.

'I'm afraid that was just me, jumping to conclusions,' she admitted reluctantly at last. 'You see, I looked in the holiday book at work and found that Zoe had had the same two weeks' holiday as you, and I suppose...I just put two and two together...'

'And came up with five...' He was smiling again.

She nodded. Her cheeks, she could tell, were now quite pink with embarrassment and she wished she could just sink into the ground.

He was silent for a moment, staring into his glass and swirling the last of the contents around. Casually, he said, 'But you wanted to know?'

'What?' she said nervously.

'You wanted to know whether we'd been away together. Was that just idle curiosity—or did you have some other reason?'

'What other reason could I possibly have had?' She raised her eyebrows in an attempt at coolness, but at the same time she was only too aware that her cheeks were still warm and gave her away.

'Could it be that it was because you cared?' he said softly.

When she didn't answer he leaned forward again. He was so close that their hands were almost touching across the table, so close that under the table his knee was against hers. 'Did you, Siobhan?' he asked looking into her eyes. 'Did you care?'

'I suppose I must have done,' she admitted at last. 'But…well, when I found out that Zoe was married it put a quite different slant on things. It was bad enough when I thought you were just chatting up two of us at the same time…'

'I guess that just about confirmed everything you'd ever heard about me? Isn't that right?' There was mischief in his eyes now.

'Well, yes.' Siobhan was also forced to laugh because what he was saying was perfectly true.

'So,' he went on, still in the same soft tones, 'you started to go off me when you thought I might be capable of breaking up a marriage—is that right?'

'Something like that—yes,' Siobhan muttered.

'But that was then. How about now? How about now that you know the truth—that I didn't take Zoe to Tenerife with me. That I, in fact, took my sister and her kids? Doesn't that put another, entirely different slant on things?' The hint of mischief in the green eyes had turned to amusement now.

'Well, yes. I suppose it might.' Siobhan nodded. She hesitated, then asked, 'So are you saying there's never been anything between you and Zoe Grainger?'

'Ah. I was waiting for that.'

'Really?' This time she achieved, she hoped, just the required degree of coolness in her tone.

'Yes, because that's a different matter altogether.' He leaned back in his chair again.

'You mean there was? Once something between you, I mean?'

He nodded. 'Yes,' he said. 'Zoe and I were at school together. And yes, we did used to go out with each other at one time. Nothing came of it and some time later she met and married Mal Grainger. End of story, as far as I was concerned.'

He paused just long enough for Siobhan to think that really could be the end of the story, but he carried on. 'Years later she came to work at the station. There were rumours that she was going through a bad time, that her marriage was breaking up. Like a fool, I provided the proverbial shoulder to cry on—but only as an old friend. You have to believe that, Siobhan, that's all it was. Anyway, I took her out a few times to try to cheer her up and, as far as I was concerned, that was that.'

He began toying with a beermat on the table before him. Glancing across at Siobhan again, he said, 'Obviously, from what you've said, it would seem Zoe read rather more into it. Anyway, my holiday came along and when I returned I found you had arrived. The rest you know.'

'Oh,' she said faintly. 'Oh, I see.'

'Do you believe me?' he asked.

She allowed her eyes to meet his. 'Yes,' she said. 'I do.'

'Good,' he said, 'because it's important to me that you do.' He put down the beermat and leaned forward across the table.

'You see,' he went on at last, 'I want us to start again from the beginning—to pretend we've just met. We seem to have been at cross purposes since that moment I walked into the station and saw you sitting there.'

'Yes, we have rather.' She smiled.

'I fancied you then,' said Dave honestly, 'and I fancy you now—so can we do what I said and start again?'

'Why not?' Siobhan laughed and gave a little shrug.

'Right, well, in that case, I'm David Morey. I'm single, unattached, twenty-nine years old and I want to know if you'll come out with me.'

'Hello, Dave,' she said. 'My name is Siobhan Catherine O'Mara. I, too, am single and unattached. I am twenty-one years old and I would like nothing better than to go out with you.'

He leaned forward again and this time their hands did touch. This time his fingers interlocked with hers. A delicious little thrill shot straight through Siobhan and Zoe's warning ceased to have any meaning. Helen's warning became little more than an echo.

'Siobhan, I can't believe what I'm hearing. I really can't.' Helen stared at her in obvious dismay. 'You're not serious. You can't be.'

'Afraid I am.' Siobhan hung her head in mock shame.

'You mean to tell me, after all I've said, that you're actually going out with him?'

Siobhan nodded, while Chester, sensing some sort of tension in the air, put his paw on her knee.

It was Sunday morning and Siobhan had gone across to The Coach House to inquire after Uncle Harry, who had been very poorly again during the last few days.

It had been after Helen had reported that there was no change in her father's condition that she'd given Siobhan a strange look and had asked her if it had been Dave Morey's car she'd seen, bringing her home, the previous night. This in turn had brought about Siobhan's confession.

'I think you may be mistaken about him,' Siobhan said a moment later. 'He's nice, you know.'

'I know he is,' Helen sighed. 'I told *you* that. He is nice. Anyone will tell you that. He has a heart of gold.'

'Well, then…'

'He will also love you and leave you, Siobhan. I've seen it all before. He seems to have the knack of making girls fall head over heels in love with him. There's a period of intense passion and then that's it…the girl is left with a broken heart and Dave Morey is ready to move on to the next one. He seems incapable of sustaining a permanent relationship.' Helen stared at her. 'You're not thinking you might be the one to change all that? Because if you are…'

'No, of course I'm not,' Siobhan interrupted. 'I'm not under any illusion of that sort—really, I'm not. I shall just enjoy it while it lasts. And, don't worry, Helen, I'm perfectly able to take care of myself. I don't intend letting anyone break my heart.'

'Hmm.' Helen sounded unconvinced but with a sigh which might have signified anything from resignation to exasperation she said, 'I suppose you're seeing him today?'

'Yes.' Siobhan nodded happily. 'We're going to the beach. He's picking me up in a few minutes' time—Oh!' They both swung round and looked out of the kitchen window as a car suddenly seemed to erupt into the drive. 'Here he comes now.' She jumped to her feet and hurried to open the door, in her haste almost tripping over Chester who seemed in as much of a hurry as herself to welcome their visitor.

'Hi, there!' Dave called through the open car window

when he caught sight of Siobhan. He brought the car to a halt with a squeal of tyres as they crunched on the loose gravel.

'Hello.' Her heart gave that funny little flip it seemed to do every time she saw him these days.

He opened his door and got out, checking as he did so that the windsurfing equipment on his roof-rack was secure. 'Morning, Helen.' He smiled and nodded.

'Good morning, Dave,' Helen replied, her expression definitely now one of resignation.

'Lovely day,' he added, apparently unperturbed by this slightly frosty reception.

'That rather depends to what you are referring,' she said. Looking at Siobhan, she added, 'Well, enjoy your windsurfing—I'll see you later.'

'Yes, all right. Love to Uncle Harry. Bye, now, Helen.' Lightly Siobhan ran round to the passenger side of Dave's car and got in, tossing her beach-bag into the rear seat as she did so.

He turned his head and smiled at her. 'You fit?' he said.

'You bet,' she replied.

'Then let's go.' He let out the clutch and winked at Helen, who stood watching them with one hand on Chester's collar.

'She doesn't approve,' he said, as they roared away down the drive.

'She says you'll love me and leave me.'

'As if I would,' he said with mock severity.

'As if,' she agreed.

Happily she settled down in her seat. The sun was shining, the sky seemed abnormally blue, the sea was beckoning them and the man beside her was exciting. The idea of him leaving her, and the misery that might bring, seemed at that moment as unlikely as a sudden snowstorm, and something that Siobhan was not prepared to even contemplate.

She knew Helen's attitude arose only out of concern because she felt a certain responsibility towards her but Siobhan also felt Helen was being overly cautious, especially as she herself had agreed just how nice Dave was.

And he was nice, she thought, casting a surreptitious glance at him from beneath her lashes. There was certainly no doubt about that.

She'd had a marvellous time during the last few days since he'd first asked her out. They'd spent practically every spare moment together, as well, of course, as their time at work. As she'd implied to Helen, she'd enjoyed every minute of it because Dave was such good company.

What she hadn't told Helen was that since the first time he'd kissed her there had been a very real danger that she *was* falling in love with him.

She thought she would probably remember that first kiss for as long as she lived. It had been during their first date when he had taken her to Freshwater in the west of the Island and they'd walked to the top of Tennyson Down. It had been a beautiful evening and the views from the top of the down, of the mainland on the one side and the English Channel on the other, had been quite breathtaking.

'Did you know,' he'd said, slipping one arm around her as they'd gazed out to sea, 'that if you sailed from here in a south-westerly direction the first land you would come to would be Brazil?'

'I'll remember that next time I'm windsurfing.' She'd laughed and leaned against him.

He'd tilted her chin, lifting her face towards him. His kiss had been gentle, tender, but with just enough hint of passion and excitement to leave Siobhan longing for the next one. And there had, of course, been others, many others, each a little more demanding, a little more exciting than the one before.

And here they were now, with a long, glorious day of sea and sun stretching before them. There was, as far as Siobhan could see, only one faint cloud on the horizon—if you discounted Helen's disapproval—and that was the possibility of Zoe's presence at the beach. When she voiced her concern to Dave his reply, although reassuring, was slightly surprising.

'I've had a word with Zoe,' he said.

'Have you?' She threw him a quick glance but his face was expressionless.

'Yes.'

'What did you say?'

'It doesn't matter,' he said shortly, 'but you needn't have any more worries in that respect. She knows the score now—she did all along, but she might have been under a misapprehension. So, in case she was, I've set the record straight.'

'Oh, I see.' Siobhan was relieved, but she found she was still a bit anxious about seeing Zoe. They'd seen each other at work, of course, since she and Dave had started going out together, but Zoe hadn't known then. 'Best to keep a low profile at work,' Dave had said. 'Ted gets twitchy about that sort of thing, especially if the couple concerned are on the same vehicle.'

That had been fairly easy, but she wasn't sure they would be able to keep it quiet during a whole day at the beach. Touching was the problem. They just couldn't seem to help themselves—that, and looking at each other at every conceivable opportunity.

As it turned out, Siobhan need not have worried because Zoe wasn't there that day and neither was Josh. She heard someone say that they were on duty that weekend. It left the day gloriously free from any tensions, totally carefree—one of those wonderful, golden days that became etched in one's memory for all time.

'Dave, Ted said he wants to see you—and you, Siobhan, as soon as you got back.'

'Right, Monica, thanks.' Dave nodded at the secretary. Turning to Siobhan, he pulled a face. 'No prizes for guessing what it's all about,' he said. 'I would say the proverbial balloon's gone up, wouldn't you?'

'Oh, dear.' She stared at him, suddenly alarmed. 'What do you think will happen?'

'I expect we're both for the chop,' he said, making a throat-cutting gesture with one hand. Catching sight of her horrified expression, he laughed and said, 'Relax, it won't be that bad. Ted can't afford to lose two qualified paras in one fell swoop.'

Siobhan, however, was far from reassured. During the last tumultuous days, as she'd fallen headlong in love with Dave, she'd given little thought to much else. She'd carried out her duties, she hoped, with as much diligence as before but, she had to confess, she hadn't bothered about the rule of relationships among members of the crews. Now it seemed it could be about to be brought home to them in the worst possible way.

As they sat outside Ted Carter's office, waiting to go in, Siobhan found that her hands were shaking. How would she cope with the humiliation if she was dismissed? How could she go home and explain it to her family?

How could she have been so foolish?

But, then, how could she have stopped herself falling in love with Dave? She certainly hadn't set out to fall in love. Somehow it had just happened—had crept up on her and taken her unawares. Turning her head, she looked at Dave and found that he was watching her. There was a look of such tenderness in his eyes that she had to swallow the lump that suddenly came to her throat.

Stretching out his hand, he took one of her trembling ones and comfortingly enclosed it. Unfortunately, at that moment the office door opened and, instead of Monica, Ted Carter himself came out to call them inside. His gaze immediately went to their hands. Siobhan expected Dave to hastily withdraw his, but he didn't. Instead, he looked steadfastly at the chief.

'Right, come on, you two—inside,' said Ted. His tone sounded more resigned than annoyed.

They stood up and Dave squeezed her hand tightly before letting it go, and they followed Ted into his office to face the music.

He came straight to the point, staring levelly at the two of them as they stood before his desk. 'It's been brought to my attention,' he said and Siobhan found herself wondering by whom, 'that the pair of you are involved in an intimate relationship. Is that correct?'

'Yes, sir,' said Dave.

Siobhan nodded, afraid that if she tried to speak her voice might have disappeared altogether.

'You know my ruling on this sort of thing?' Ted was looking at Dave as he spoke, as if he held him more responsible than he did Siobhan.

'Yes.' Dave nodded.

'Do you have anything to say about it?'

'Only that it wasn't planned,' Dave replied quietly. 'It just happened, didn't it?' He half turned to Siobhan.

'Oh, yes,' she said, and her voice came out as little more than a whisper. 'It certainly wasn't planned. It was the last thing I thought would happen.'

'Hmm.' Ted, who must have heard similar explanations dozens of times before, stared at them with a mixture of exasperation that they had put him in such a position and thoughtfulness as to how he should cope with it. He began drumming his fingers on the desk. 'I can't just let it go,' he said at last.

'No, of course not,' Dave agreed.

'After all, rules are rules.'

'Absolutely,' said Dave.

Ted looked up quickly, narrowing his eyes slightly as if he suspected that Dave might be taking a rise out of him, but Dave's face was expressionless.

Ted stood up and walked to a large planner that took up one entire wall of his office. For the next few minutes, with his back to them and in total silence, he proceeded to study it. The only sound in the office was the ticking of the wall clock, and from outside the distant hum of activity from the rest of the station.

Just when Siobhan's nerves had reached screaming point and she thought she wouldn't be able to bear another moment, Ted turned and walked back to the desk.

'I'm going to change the crews,' he said at last.

Dave sucked in his breath.

'Unfortunately, I can't do it immediately because rotas and shifts have been set for the next couple of weeks,' Ted went on, 'but after that you, Siobhan, will go with Josh Meecher and Dave will go with Greg Freeman. I can't put Greg with Zoe because he's too inexperienced to go with a non-paramedic. That leaves Zoe Grainger with Barry Weston.'

He paused, peering at the two of them over the top of his glasses, then said, 'Barry won't like it, but it can't be helped. I'm not happy about this, I'll be perfectly frank with you. It's caused a lot of trouble and, as a team, I'd had nothing but good reports about you two, but...' He sighed. 'I suppose these things happen. At least it isn't as if either of you is married—that would have been a lot more difficult to sort out. As it is, I can't let things continue the way they are because I fear patients' welfare may be put at risk so this rearrangement is the only other option.'

'Well, it could have been a lot worse,' said Dave a few minutes later when they found themselves outside in the corridor once more.

'Yes, I suppose so,' said Siobhan slowly. 'At least we still have our jobs, but I wonder...who told him?'

'Who do you think?'

'You mean...?' She shot him a glance. 'Not Zoe?'

'I would say there's a very good chance.'

'But surely...?'

'A woman scorned and all that.'

'Yes, but would she be that vindictive?'

'Quite possibly. Don't forget I know her of old.'

'Yes, but...' She shook her head, not wanting to believe that anyone could do that sort of thing to colleagues, especially colleagues for whom one has professed friendship and, in Dave's case, something more. She was about to say as much to Dave when, to her surprise, he gave a chuckle.

'What is it?' she said, amazed there was anything he could find funny in the situation.

'I think we've just tasted a bit of poetic justice,' he said.

'What do you mean?' she asked curiously. They had just reached the door of the crew room and Dave stopped, peering through the glass portal to see who was inside before they went in.

'Well,' he said, 'you'll be OK with old Josh, won't you?'

'Yes,' she said doubtfully, 'but I'd much rather be with you.'

'I know,' he said, 'and I with you, but in the circumstances there's not a lot we can do about it. I think Ted might have turned a blind eye if we hadn't let it interfere with our work, but once it was officially pointed out to him it was a different matter.'

'Greg's a good worker, isn't he?' Siobhan interrupted him anxiously.

'Oh, yes, I'll be OK with Greg. But just think—Zoe's ended up with Barry. I would say they just about deserve each other, wouldn't you?'

CHAPTER TEN

'GOOD morning, Doc,' Dave nodded at the tall, fair-haired man who opened the front door to them.

'Hello, Dave.' The man nodded at Siobhan, before standing back to allow them into the house. 'It's rather a mess in here, I'm afraid,' he said. 'The lady has become something of a recluse. She's had a CVA and is in renal failure. I hope you like cats,' he added drily.

As Siobhan stepped into the front room of the old farm cottage the stench suddenly hit her, and she almost gagged. It took her a few seconds to get her bearings as the light from the one small window was barely adequate. The smell was a pungent mixture of urine, vomit and decay, all with an underlying strong animal odour.

She stood in the centre of the small room and peered around her. It was sparsely furnished but the bare wooden table was littered with rotting food, over which a mass of bluebottles crawled.

The patient, a very elderly lady with straggly grey hair, was lying on a threadbare couch drawn up in front of a two-bar electric fire, which was on full in spite of the fact that it was mid-summer. The lady was covered with a grey woollen blanket, which looked as if it had hosted a party for the entire local moth population.

A movement in one dim corner of the room suddenly caught Siobhan's eye and, turning sharply, she saw them. They were everywhere—on the chairs, on top of a cupboard, on the sideboard, on the couch at the patient's feet. There was even one on the mantelpiece.

Tabby cats, ginger cats, kittens, grey cats, a black cat and, even as Siobhan stared in astonishment, the matriarch of them all, a huge white cat which jumped onto the table. The bluebottles buzzed furiously and the cat began to lick the remains of what once might have been a chicken.

'Oh, God,' muttered Dave, momentarily transfixed as he gazed around in shocked amazement. 'I thought I'd seen it all in this job. Who called you, Doc?'

'The police,' said the doctor, taking the oxygen that Dave passed to him. Crouching beside the old lady, he placed the mask over her face. 'Apparently, the postman called, couldn't get any reply, came back the next day and when he still couldn't raise her he contacted the police. They broke in and found her on the floor.'

'Poor soul,' said Siobhan. 'I'll get a stretcher.'

She was glad to escape—to get outside where, thankfully, she drew in great lungfuls of the fresh air. It was raining that day, that fine steady drizzle in which one quickly becomes wet, but Siobhan hardly noticed as she collected a stretcher and blankets from the ambulance.

Inevitably the moment came when she had to go back into the cottage. Taking a deep breath, she dived inside.

'...get her in as soon as we can,' the doctor was saying to Dave.

'Does she have anyone else?' asked Dave.

'There's no one local mentioned in her records,' the doctor replied. 'Next of kin and executor of her will is a distant cousin, living in Scotland.'

Between them they lifted the patient onto the stretcher, where Siobhan tucked the blankets around her.

'It's a severe stroke,' said the doctor as he switched off the electric fire. 'Loss of speech and paralysis.'

'What about the cats?' asked Dave, glancing over his shoulder with a slight shudder.

'I rang the local branch of the Cats' Protection League and informed them. They are going to send someone over. I've opened several tins of food and there's plenty of water. I'll drop the keys into Social Services.'

The doctor accompanied them to the ambulance. After checking that his patient was as comfortable as possible he said, 'She's all yours. I'll get back to the centre now.'

'Cheers, Dr Hammond,' said Dave.

When Siobhan had closed the ambulance doors on Dave and the patient, she turned to the doctor.

'You're Dr Hammond?' she asked. She'd wondered who he was when they'd first arrived, assuming because she hadn't seen him before that he might be from one of the neighbouring practices.

'That's right.' He'd been about to get into his car, which was parked on the grass behind the ambulance, but he paused and stared keenly at Siobhan. 'And you,' he went on, as if it had only just dawned on him, 'must be Siobhan O'Mara—Helen's cousin.'

'That's me.' Siobhan smiled. 'I believe we have a flat in common.'

'We have, indeed.' He laughed. 'The good old stable flat. It did me a good turn, I can tell you.'

'And me,' replied Siobhan.

'Do you intend staying there?'

'For the time being,' she replied. 'At least until I find something more permanent.'

'You will.' He laughed again. 'Look what happened to me.' With a wave, he got into his car and reversed. Siobhan raised her hand in response as he drew away, then she climbed into the driver's seat of the ambulance.

'Nice chap, Jon Hammond,' called Dave from the rear.

'Yes, very,' Siobhan agreed as she started the engine. 'I would say he and Kate Chapman make a very good pair. It sounds as if it was all very romantic, her being one of the partners and him being a locum.'

'Bit like us,' said Dave, and she could hear the laughter in his voice.

'If you like,' she replied. 'Although I doubt anyone at the centre told them they shouldn't be having a relationship because they happen to be working together.'

'No, I bet they didn't.' He paused. 'You know something?' he went on after a moment. 'I've been really good today, trying to put it from my mind, concentrating on my work and all that, and what happens? Talking like that, you've got me going again. Where are we going tonight?'

'Were we going anywhere?' she asked coolly as, flicking the switch for the blues, she swung the vehicle out of the rutted farm track and into the lane.

'I don't know,' he replied, 'but I can tell you one thing—we sure as hell are now.'

He took her to a little seafood restaurant, overlooking the Solent. The rain of earlier had stopped around midday and the afternoon had been warm and sunny, ending with a quite spectacular sunset that left the high mackerel sky bathed in a deep crimson wash.

They ate mussels, followed by fresh sea bream in a prawn sauce together with a lightly tossed green salad and washed down with a crisp, dry Muscadet.

Both were conscious that the awareness between them had steadily grown in the last few days and was rapidly approaching fever pitch.

As they ate their meal they gave only cursory glances to the scene outside—the darkening waters of the Solent with its shipping activity, yachts returning to night moorings, ferries, lighted now as dusk approached, or the occasional liner on the distant skyline as it returned to Southampton from some far-flung, exotic location—because they only had eyes for each other.

Later, when they slipped away from the restaurant and returned to Dave's car, Siobhan leaned against him in the darkness and gave herself up to the thrill of his kiss.

'You know something, Siobhan?' he said at last as, with a deep sigh, he drew away from her. 'I think you've utterly bewitched me with your Irish charm.'

'Why do you say that?' she whispered, reaching out one hand and lightly touching his cheek.

'I'll tell you why.' He caught her hand and pressed it to his mouth, teasing her fingers between his teeth. 'It's because I've never felt quite like this ever before. You must have cast some Celtic spell on me, Siobhan O'Mara, because I do believe I'm in love with you.'

'I love you, too,' she whispered. 'I can hardly believe it. I never thought it could happen in such a short space of time, but it has…' She trailed off as he silenced her, encasing her face between his hands, his fingers hopelessly entangled in her cloud of hair as his mouth found hers, his tongue questing, parting her lips as a shaft of hot desire ran through her body.

As his kiss grew deeper it grew more demanding, and his hands moved from her face to her body, growing even more urgent as they moulded her breasts, moving down over her hips and thighs.

'Siobhan.' His voice was husky, thick with desire. 'I want you so much.'

She didn't answer. Part of her, the reckless part,

wanted him desperately—wanted him to relieve that throbbing desire deep inside her—but…another part, the sensible part, warned it would be folly to do so.

Mistaking her silence for assent, Dave made as if to start the car's engine.

With a supreme effort Siobhan got herself under control. Taking a deep breath, she put a restraining hand on his arm. 'No, Dave,' she said quietly.

He turned his head to look at her.

'No…?' he said, and there was no mistaking the surprise in his voice.

'No.' She shook her head.

'But why? Why not?' She could see his puzzled expression in the half-light, hear the bewilderment in his voice.

'Because…because I imagine you intend going to your flat?'

'Well, yes. I didn't think you'd want to go to The Coach House…'

'No, but neither should we go to your flat, Dave—because if we do,' she said quickly, 'there would be a very good chance we would end up in bed together…'

'Well…yes.' He paused. 'Would that be so terrible?'

'I don't want that to happen, Dave,' she said quietly.

'You don't…?' He stared at her, obviously at a loss to know what to say.

She drew another breath. 'If I came back to your flat with you, knowing I don't intend for this to go any further, it simply wouldn't be fair…especially to you. I understand there is a name for girls who do that sort of thing and I certainly wouldn't want that label attached to me…' She trailed off, aware that she was beginning to waffle and that Dave was still staring at her in puzzled amazement.

'What is it?' she said at last in a small voice.

He shook his head. 'I'm not sure I understand,' he said.

'Not sure you understand what?'

'Well,' he said slowly, carefully, 'I thought we'd agreed that we love each other?'

'Yes.' She nodded in agreement.

'In which case I assumed... No.' He hesitated briefly. 'I'll rephrase that. I *hoped* that the next logical stage would be to—'

'Sleep together?'

'I was going to say, to show and to prove our love for each other,' he said.

'That's what I said.' She nodded. 'To sleep together.'

'If you prefer, all right, to sleep together. What's wrong with that?'

'Oh, there's nothing wrong with it,' said Siobhan hastily. 'Nothing wrong whatsoever. It's just that...I don't.'

They were parked beneath a streetlamp, and in its glow she saw his eyes widen slightly.

'You don't what?' he said.

'Sleep around,' she said firmly.

He let out his breath with a long drawn-out sound. 'Siobhan,' he said, 'I'm not exactly asking you to sleep around. I'm only wanting you to sleep with me.'

When she remained silent he went on gently, 'It's not so terrible, you know. It's what people do when they love each other.'

'It's what married people do,' she said quietly.

'Well, yes, that's true.' After a long moment of silence he added, 'But these days it's what a lot of other people do as well.' He paused. 'Let's face it, Siobhan, if you didn't and then you got married and it was a complete and utter disaster in that department you'd only have yourself to blame, wouldn't you?'

'You mean, one should sample the merchandise?' said Siobhan. 'And if it's found wanting in any way it should be rejected?'

'I didn't mean to sound quite as mercenary as that,' protested Dave.

They fell silent again, an uncomfortable silence this time in which the only sound to be heard was the occasional noise of a passing car.

At last, picking up her hand, he pressed it against his face. 'I'm sorry,' he said. 'I didn't mean to offend you, I really didn't. It's just that I love you and I want you. To me that is perfectly natural and quite normal.'

'I know.' She rested her face against his hand. 'And I feel the same way.'

'I'm relieved to hear it.' He gave a long deep sigh. 'So now can we...?'

'Dave...' She drew away and looked at him in the darkness. 'Let me try and explain something to you. I'm not sure you will understand, but I would like you to try.'

'Go on,' he said uncertainly, as if afraid at what he might be about to hear.

'A long time ago,' she said, 'I made a decision...a sort of pact with myself that I wasn't going to sleep with anyone until I got married. I want it to be special, you see.' She paused for a long moment, then added, 'And I want to keep that pact.'

There was a slightly stunned silence, then slowly Dave said, 'You mean...you haven't? Not with anyone? Ever?' He sounded so incredulous that she couldn't help smiling.

'No,' she said, 'I haven't. Not with anyone. Ever.'

'But…but…what about boyfriends?' He was quite obviously astounded. 'Surely you've had other boyfriends…a lovely girl like you?'

'Oh, yes, dozens.' She smiled again.

'So what happened when they wanted to…?'

'I told them exactly the same as I've told you.'

'And what were their reactions?'

'A bit like yours, I suppose. Some simply couldn't cope—I never saw those again—and others, well, others just carried on with the relationship until it fizzled out. I knew then they simply weren't right, weren't meant to be.'

'So this isn't anything to do with me personally?' He sounded relieved.

'Of course not,' she said quickly. 'Although…' She hesitated.

'Yes…what?' he said suspiciously.

'There is one difference.'

'And what's that?'

'I didn't really love any of them.'

'Oh,' he said. 'Oh, I see.'

He fell silent again, gazing out of his car window towards the lights on the distant shore of the mainland, as if trying to come to terms with what she had said.

Siobhan wondered what he was thinking. At last, after she'd waited in an agony of silence, he turned his head and looked straight ahead.

'I'm not sure I do understand, Siobhan,' he said. 'To be honest with you, I didn't think anyone felt that way any more. But I…I'll respect your decision.'

'Thank you,' she replied, waiting—hoping—he would turn towards her this time and take her in his arms, kiss her, tell her it didn't matter—that he still loved her, anyway.

Instead, he leaned forward and started the engine.

'I think,' he said, 'I'd better take you home.'

Her heart sank. It was what she'd heard so many times before on other occasions, with other boyfriends, when they'd learnt she wasn't about to jump into bed with them. But they had been different because, as she'd tried to explain to Dave, she hadn't really loved any of them and certainly hadn't wanted to marry any of them.

Now she'd found someone she did love, someone she was beginning to think she could happily spend the rest of her life with—and he wasn't the marrying kind.

Through a mist of tears the lights on the distant shore blurred into a single line.

There was a slight coolness between them again. To an outsider it would have been barely perceptible, but to Siobhan it was very real. She hoped at first it might simply be that Dave was uncertain how to handle the situation and that he would eventually come to accept it, but as the days passed she began to fear that for them it might well signify the beginning of the end.

The one person who might have noticed something untoward was Helen and she, predictably, was the one to mention it to Siobhan.

It happened early one evening after Siobhan had returned from work and Helen came across to the stable flat with a parcel that had been left that morning at The Coach House for Siobhan.

'The postman probably didn't want to leave it in the open so he put it in the porch where he leaves anything that arrives for me during the day,' said Helen. As she handed over the parcel she said, 'It's from Ireland.'

'Oh,' said Siobhan. 'Thank you—it's from Mum.' She looked down at the stamps and her mother's familiar handwriting and, because she'd been feeling low and a bit confused by mixed emotions, the tears sprang to her eyes.

This didn't, of course, go unnoticed by Helen, who threw her a keen glance, shut the door behind her and came right into the kitchen. 'What is it?' she said.

'Oh, it's nothing,' said Siobhan. 'Just a bit of homesickness, that's all. Seeing Mum's writing…' Dashing her tears furiously away with the back of her hand, she turned and led the way into her sitting room.

'Homesickness, you say?' said Helen, following her. 'So why don't I believe you?'

'I don't know…' Siobhan trailed off, unable to continue—afraid she wouldn't be able to negotiate the huge lump in her throat.

'It's him, isn't it—Dave bloody Morey?' said Helen grimly.

'Don't call him that,' said Siobhan faintly. 'It really isn't his fault.' She sank down onto the sofa.

'So tell me whose fault it is if it isn't his?' demanded Helen. When Siobhan gave a helpless little shrug she said, 'I heard via the grapevine that you two were being separated at work—is that correct?'

Siobhan nodded miserably.

'How did that come about?'

'Someone told Ted Carter that Dave and I were having a relationship. Ted doesn't allow that among two members of the same crew so he's decided to separate us in a week or so's time.'

'So is that the cause of all this misery?' Helen looked faintly surprised.

'No,' said Siobhan. 'No, of course not.' She hesitated.

'So what is it?' Helen peered at her. 'He's not two-timing you, is he? Because, if he is, I'll—'

'No, Helen.' Siobhan sighed. 'He isn't two-timing me—really, he isn't. It's nothing like that.'

'Then what?' Helen frowned.

'I just don't think it's going to work out, that's all. We have different ideas about relationships...' She broke off, uncertain how to continue—how she could put it into words—afraid Helen wouldn't understand any more than Dave had.

'He expected you to sleep with him, didn't he?' The bluntness of the question almost took Siobhan's breath away. She was about to deny it, but she shrugged. What did it matter? What did any of it matter now?

'And you don't want to,' said Helen shrewdly. 'That's it, isn't it?'

'Not quite,' said Siobhan. 'The fact is, yes, I do want to. Very much. But...' she shrugged again '...I made a pact with myself that I wouldn't, at least not until I had found the right man—the man I wanted to spend the rest of my life with.'

'And that certainly isn't Dave Morey,' said Helen quickly. When Siobhan remained silent she threw her another quick, startled glance. 'I take it it isn't?'

Siobhan took a deep breath. Getting to her feet, she went to the window where she stood looking out at the garden with unseeing eyes.

At last she turned to Helen again. 'I don't know,' she whispered, 'but I think he might be.'

'Oh, Siobhan.' Helen stared at her, then in a slightly flat voice said, 'You're in love with him.'

'Yes,' she replied shakily. 'I think I must be.'

'After all my warnings...'

'I know, but it just happened. I couldn't help it.'

'And what about him?'

Siobhan shook her head. 'I don't know. I'm not sure.

I thought he felt the same way, but I don't know how he'll cope with my not sleeping with him...'

'If he loves you—' Helen began heatedly.

'I know,' said Siobhan quickly. 'Oh, I know all that, but I think he must imagine I'm some sort of freak. He obviously isn't used to it. But if I do I fear it might be as you said—he'll love me, then leave me and move on... He's already made it quite plain he isn't interested in long-term or permanent commitment.'

'So, how's he been since you told him?' asked Helen after a moment.

'Cool,' said Siobhan. 'Yes, that's the only word to describe it—cool. Like I said, I guess he thinks I must be some sort of freak—either that or he's come to the conclusion I must be frigid.'

'If he understood your background...your upbringing,' muttered Helen, half to herself, 'maybe he would understand.'

'I'm not sure any of that has anything to do with it,' said Siobhan. 'This is me—the way I feel, the way I want things to be between myself and the man I eventually marry. The decision was mine and mine alone, and had nothing whatsoever to do with anyone else.'

'Well, I admire you,' said Helen. 'There can't be many these days that have standards like that—and stick to them when the going gets tough.'

'I must admit,' Siobhan gave a faint smile, 'the last few days have made me wonder whether my ideas are hopelessly outdated and I'm simply out of step with everyone else.'

'You hang on in there,' said Helen, 'and it'll all come right in the end. You'll see.' She turned to go but Siobhan, suddenly remembering something, called her back.

'Oh, Helen,' she said, 'do you have any idea what happened to that lady we brought in a few days ago? The one who'd had the CVA?'

'You mean Miss Winterton? The cat lady?'

'Yes, that's her. She was in a bit of a bad way when she was found.'

'Yes,' Helen agreed. 'I understand she's very ill.'

'Poor lady,' said Siobhan. 'Didn't anyone ever visit her?'

'She didn't want anyone, apparently,' Helen replied. 'She refused to let anyone in. She'd become something of a recluse in that cottage, with only her cats for company.'

'The cats were everywhere,' said Siobhan, 'and I must say they seemed very well cared-for. I dare say she spent all her pension on them rather than on herself.'

'You could be right,' said Helen.

'Any idea what happened to them?'

'I heard that it took two men from the Cats' Protection League and a couple more from the RSPCA to round them all up. Some of them were quite wild, it seems.'

'Do you think Miss Winterton will be able to go back there—to her cottage?' asked Siobhan.

Helen shook her head. 'It seems highly unlikely. If she survives the stroke, which is doubtful, she would never be able to manage on her own.'

'She'd hate it living in a residential unit after being alone for so long,' said Siobhan.

Helen nodded. 'Yes, I would imagine it'd come very hard.'

'Almost as hard as someone who is used to living with someone else suddenly finding themselves alone...' As soon as she'd spoken Siobhan realised what she'd said. 'Oh, Helen,' she said. 'I'm sorry. I wasn't thinking.'

'It's OK,' said Helen gently. 'I'm starting to get used to it without Dad now, although I must admit it was very hard at first. I kept thinking I'd forgotten to do something, like get him a meal. I'd get into quite a panic before I remembered I didn't have to do it any more.' She sighed, then said, 'Oh, well, I suppose I'd better go, that is...' she stared at Siobhan again '...if you're sure you're all right.'

'Oh, yes,' said Siobhan, 'I'm fine. Really, I am.'

But after Helen had gone another glance at her mother's handwriting once again brought the tears to her eyes.

CHAPTER ELEVEN

'So won't you be going to tonight's barbeque at all?' Greg Freeman looked from Siobhan to Dave and back to Siobhan again.

'Yes,' said Dave, 'when we've finished our shift. We don't all have Saturday night off, you know.' He paused and peered keenly at Greg. 'Who are you taking to the barbeque, Greg?'

'What do you mean?' A slow flush began to creep up from Greg's neck to his face.

'Well, I heard a whisper that it might be a certain little receptionist from the Fleetwood Centre. Now, could that be right?' There was a teasing note in Dave's voice as he called across the crew room.

'It might be,' mumbled Greg, the flush spreading to the very roots of his blond hair.

'Is that Claire or Jackie?' called another crew member, picking up on the banter.

'At a guess, I'd say it was Jackie,' said Josh Meecher, joining in the general teasing of the new young paramedic. 'Got quite a thing about redheads, haven't you, Greg?' As he said it everyone looked at Siobhan, and to her dismay she felt her own cheeks grow hot.

At that moment someone shouted that a couple of calls had just come in, and Dave and Josh went off to the control room. The crew room began to clear and briefly Siobhan found herself alone with Greg.

'Is that right about you and Jackie?' she asked, smiling at him.

He nodded, a little sheepishly. 'Yes,' he admitted. 'I have asked her to go with me.' He paused. 'I guess you'll be going with Dave?'

He said it half-ruefully but as if he'd already come to terms with that particular situation. Siobhan, however, had no time to answer for at that moment the doors were flung open again and Dave stood there.

'Come on, Siobhan,' he called. 'This one's for us.'

'See you, Greg,' she called over her shoulder as she ran to join Dave.

'Yes…' Greg replied a little wistfully. 'See you.'

'So, what is it?' Siobhan asked, as she and Dave scrambled aboard their ambulance.

'A call from the Blackgang Chine area in the south of the Island,' Dave replied as he started the engine. 'Apparently, there's an injured woman somewhere on a site under the cliffs. Heaven knows how she got there or, for that matter, how we're supposed to reach her.'

'What do you mean?' Siobhan threw him a glance.

'There have been a lot of landfalls at Blackgang Chine in recent years,' Dave replied. 'After severe storms great chunks of land have quite literally slipped away into the sea. I remember once part of the road fell away, taking some houses with it.'

'Was anyone killed?' asked Siobhan.

'No,' he replied. 'Fortunately, residents were evacuated in time.'

'Do we know what's happened to this particular woman?'

Dave shook his head. 'No,' he said. 'Simply that she's injured. At a guess, I would say she was probably climbing and has had a fall. People will ignore the warning signs on those cliffs. The call came from a public phone box and the caller hung up before the control room could get any more details. But if she's in too inaccessible a place we'll have to send for a rescue helicopter to airlift her.'

'Really?' Siobhan looked up sharply.

'It wouldn't be the first time,' said Dave. 'Not around here, with cliff rescues and sea rescues and the like. They very often send us in first to administer the necessary first aid, then follow up with an airlift.'

'Exciting stuff,' said Siobhan.

They fell silent after that as Dave drove as fast as the narrow, twisting roads allowed. Because it was late afternoon they were hampered by holiday-makers, returning to their hotels and holiday centres after a day out in the sun.

The villages they forced their way through were congested with coaches, cars and groups of people who overflowed from the pavements and drifted across the roads.

Eventually they found themselves on the open road approaching Blackgang. It was then that Siobhan stole another glance at Dave. His face was set and determined and as she took in the contours of the face that had become so dear to her in such a surprisingly short space of time she felt a sudden rush of love for him. He had been very quiet in the past few days. Even if the coolness which had been between them had lifted slightly, he was still treating her with a politeness that led her to fear that she had lost him.

There had been no further reference to their recent conversation. While he had taken her out once since then, the evening had been somewhat stilted and at the end his goodnight kiss had been brief, with none of the fire or passion of previous ones.

It couldn't last—Siobhan knew that. He would soon

tire of the situation and move on, so proving Helen's prediction that he would love her and leave her, albeit not in quite the way Helen had foreseen.

But Siobhan wasn't sure she would be able to bear it when that happened. She loved him. She didn't want to lose him, but it seemed the only way she might not lose him would be to do as he wanted.

And maybe that was the only way, after all. Maybe she was being silly and old-fashioned, clinging to out-dated ideas.

On the other hand, if she did as he wanted and slept with him—maybe even moved in with him—what guar-antee did she have that he wouldn't tire of her anyway and move on yet again, just as he had in the past with other women?

'Here we go,' he said, suddenly breaking into her thoughts. 'Hold tight. I'm going to go down the old road just as far as I can, then we'll probably have to walk the rest of the way—or climb,' he added ominously.

They drove to a small clearing where Dave brought the ambulance to a halt and they climbed out. Tall cliffs loomed above, while below them the land fell steeply away right down to the beach where the vast blue ex-panse of the sea seemed to stretch away into eternity.

It was curiously silent, with only the occasional cries of seabirds to be heard as they swooped and circled over-head in their endless search for food. Even the wind was still that day, with not so much as a breeze to stir the dense foliage of the gorse and broom bushes on the cliff face. A single hawk hovered, its outline etched sharply against the deep blue of the sky and its wings almost motionless as it waited, preparing to swoop on some unsuspecting prey.

'The road ends here,' said Dave, arms akimbo as he

gazed around him. 'Look, you can see where it continued before that great chunk in the middle fell away
into the sea.' He pointed across a landslide of rocks and
mud to a point in the distance where the road seemed to
continue.

'So where is our patient?' asked Siobhan, also gazing
around. She felt quite strange in this heady, silent atmos-
phere, awestruck by the sheer force of nature and of
what it could do.

'That's anybody's guess,' said Dave. 'It could just as
likely have been a hoax call—we do get those.'

'Wait a minute.' Siobhan stared, then suddenly
clutched his arm. 'There's someone down there.' She
pointed to one side away from the cliffs where a large
section of the land dipped away almost out of sight,
forming what looked like a huge tunnel with the tops of
the tall trees that lined its sides meeting overhead. In the
very depths they could just make out someone moving.

'We'd better go and look,' said Dave. 'We'll take our
cases with us. I'm not risking taking the ambulance
down there—we might never get it out again.'

They collected their cases, a stretcher and blankets,
locked the ambulance and began to make their way carefully down over rocks and grassy hillocks into the cool
green darkness of the valley. It was quieter than ever
there, with even the screams of the seabirds muted.
Sunlight dappled the leaves and filtered through the
branches of the tall sycamores beside the steep pathway.

'There they are,' said Siobhan suddenly. 'There are
several people down there in that clearing.'

'Good God!' exclaimed Dave, pausing for a moment
and peering ahead of them into the valley. 'They've got
an old bus—how in the world did they manage to get
that down there?'

Cautiously they approached the clearing, which appeared to be the scene of a campsite. Two tents had been set up alongside the old bus and in the centre of the clearing were the ashes of a camp-fire.

'I've just realised who they are,' said Dave. 'They call themselves New Age travellers. I've seen them before, parked in other places. I recognise their bus now. Hello, there,' he called, as a tall, swarthy-looking man approached them. 'You have an injured woman with you, I believe?'

'This way.' The man jerked his thumb over his shoulder. As he turned and they began to follow him towards the bus Siobhan noticed his dark hair was tied back into a ponytail and his tattered trousers were bound beneath the knees with thin cord.

Other people now began to appear—two boys who kicked an empty tin can through the charred cinders of the bonfire, another man who eyed them warily, his hand on the collar of a thin-faced mongrel which growled menacingly as they grew closer, and a woman who stood on the steps of the bus with her arms folded, suspicion in her dark eyes.

'So where is she?' Dave directed the question to the man who had led them into the camp, but it was the woman on the steps who turned and silently led the way inside the vehicle.

Siobhan was aware of a beaded curtain, a narrow gangway, drapes which had once been rich in colour but were now shabby and faded, of a child with large, sad eyes who watched them with her thumb stuck firmly in her mouth and of the scent of sweet, sickly joss sticks that burned in a jar on a shelf.

Then they were in a small alcove at the very end of the bus, curtained off from the rest. A makeshift bed had been set up and a young woman lay on the grubby covers. Her long frizzy hair was damp and spread out around her on a worn velvet cushion, her face was deathly pale while her eyes, dark rimmed with kohl, appeared almost sunken in her head.

'What happened?' asked Dave. 'What are her injuries?'

When there was no reply to his question Siobhan crouched down alongside the woman. 'What is your name?' she said quietly.

'Marianne,' the woman whispered. With a little gasp she lifted back the covers, and Siobhan saw the mound that was her stomach and the bright red patch that stained the striped mattress she lay on.

'She's in labour,' Siobhan said, glancing over her shoulder.

'Why didn't anyone say?' demanded Dave.

'We didn't think you'd come if you knew,' muttered the other, older woman. 'She's not booked in anywhere.'

'Hasn't she had any treatment at all during her pregnancy?' said Siobhan.

When the woman shook her head sullenly she asked, 'But why?'

'Never needed it before. This one's different.'

'She's losing blood badly,' said Siobhan to Dave as he opened his medical case. 'I think we'd best get a cannula in and set up a drip before her veins collapse.'

After the other woman had scooped up the child and disappeared outside, Dave and Siobhan worked quickly and quietly, each anticipating the other's every move. They had barely secured the drip and the Entonox for pain relief when a strong contraction shook Marianne's swollen body.

'I don't think we can get her up to the ambulance,' muttered Dave, a hint of desperation in his voice.

'Is this one for the helicopter?' asked Siobhan.

'I'm not sure.' Dave looked worried. 'They'd never be able to land down here, and in her condition a winch is out of the question.'

'The foetal heart is still strong,' said Siobhan a moment later, 'but I don't like this bleeding. She may require a Caesarean section.'

'I'm going to get a doctor,' said Dave. Taking his mobile phone from his jacket, he made his way back through the bus to the door.

Siobhan was just wondering if there was anything else she could do to make Marianne more comfortable when the girl gave a loud cry and arched her body, at the same time gripping the covers in handfuls and twisting them as another violent contraction seized her.

'It's coming...' she gasped. 'The baby...it's coming...'

Quickly Siobhan folded back the bedclothes again and listened once more to the foetal heartbeat. To her relief, it was still strong, but at the same time Marianne had begun to push, bearing down strongly as the contractions came fast with barely a pause between them.

Mercifully the bleeding seemed to have eased, if only temporarily, and as Siobhan instructed Marianne to raise her legs she realised with a little shock that the cervix was almost fully dilated as the crown of the baby's head, with a covering of dark hair, was already clearly visible.

Carefully, she checked the drip. As another fierce contraction gripped Marianne and she cried out Siobhan passed her the Entonox mask, which had slipped to the floor. Marianne began to push again and Siobhan, aware that Dave had come back into the bus and was hovering somewhere behind her, quietly and calmly offered encouragement.

'Come on, Marianne,' she said urgently. 'Push. Now. Push. There's a good girl. I can see the baby's head. There's lots of dark hair. Come on. That's right, push again. Good. Now, I want you to pant. That's right. Short, sharp breaths. That's right, Marianne. Good girl. You're doing very well.'

She took a deep breath. 'Right, steady, now. Here's another contraction so push again. Now. No, not yet. Baby's not quite ready yet. Next time. Rest now, just for a moment. Here, let me wipe your face.' She took the moist wipe that Dave passed her and gently sponged the girl's face. 'That's better, isn't it?' she said gently.

'Yes...' whispered Marianne, grabbing Siobhan's arm and gripping it tightly as she gave a sudden gasp. 'Oh, sweet Jesus, help me. Here comes another one...'

'This time, Marianne,' said Siobhan. 'Yes, this time. Push. And again. Yes...ah...yes.'

As the baby's head was born Siobhan gently guided it into the world, turning it slightly as the shoulders emerged.

Another contraction shook Marianne and Siobhan felt Dave's hand briefly squeeze her shoulder, the gesture both encouraging and comforting, then her attention was back to the miracle unfolding before their eyes as the baby's tiny form slipped from its mother's body. Siobhan realised she had been holding her breath. She let it go now in a long drawn-out sigh.

'It's a girl,' she breathed, gazing down at the tiny, perfect, female form. 'You have a daughter, Marianne.'

'Is...is she all right?' whispered Marianne.

'Let's see now.' Dave leaned forward over Siobhan's shoulder. 'Ten fingers, ten toes—two of everything else.

Yes, she's perfect…beautiful, Marianne, just like her mother.' He paused and then, as yet another contraction gathered, murmured, 'Placenta, Siobhan.'

'What about the cord?' she murmured back. 'Should we…?'

'Best not,' said Dave. 'The doctor's on his way.'

Carefully they wrapped baby, cord and placenta in one of their clean cellular blankets, then placed the precious bundle on Marianne's body where she received it eagerly, enfolding it in her arms.

'Thank you,' she whispered. 'Oh, thank you.' Wordlessly, she gazed down at her baby.

Siobhan glanced up at Dave, but could hardly see him through the mist of tears that clouded her eyes.

'Is Marc there?' asked Marianne anxiously a moment later.

'I'll get him,' said Dave. Straightening up, he made his way down the bus.

While he was gone Siobhan checked the drip once more, knowing how important the life-saving fluid was to Marianne at this crucial time.

A few moments later Dave was back, together with the man with the ponytail who seemed to have lost his surly air as he, too, gazed down in wonder at his little daughter.

'Her name will be Briony,' said Marianne, as Marc tenderly smoothed the baby's forehead. 'We'd already decided that if it was a girl…' She hesitated, looking up at Siobhan. 'What is your name?' she asked.

'Siobhan,' she replied. 'Siobhan Catherine.'

'That's lovely.' Marianne glanced questioningly up at Marc, who slightly inclined his head in reply.

'So Briony Siobhan it is,' Marianne said firmly.

At that moment there was a slight commotion outside

the bus. Dave went to investigate and seconds later was back. 'It's the doctor,' he said. 'I guess we'd all better get out of here so he can examine mother and daughter.'

'It gets to you, doesn't it?' Dave thumped his chest. 'Right here.'

'It certainly does,' Siobhan agreed shakily, as they drove back to the ambulance station after transporting Marianne and her baby to the postnatal unit of the Shalbrooke.

'I've never thought of myself as being particularly paternal,' Dave went on after a moment, 'but seeing you there, Siobhan, holding that newborn baby, did something—I'm not sure what, but it really got to me...' He trailed off as if he was unable to complete what he was trying to say. Taking a deep breath, he went on, 'You were brilliant back there, you know.'

'Thank you,' Siobhan replied, 'but I was only doing my job.'

'Sometimes we're asked to do more than our job,' said Dave. 'I reckon this was one of those times.'

'You would have done the same,' she said.

'I like to think I would,' said Dave, 'but I've got my doubts that I would have done it as calmly and efficiently as you.'

They were mostly silent after that, but Siobhan found that her longing for Dave had intensified even more after the overwhelming events of the day.

When their shift was over, and the ambulance cleaned and put away for the night, Dave glanced at his watch. 'Are you going straight to the barbeque?' he said. 'I'm going to change here to save time.'

Siobhan hesitated. 'I've been thinking,' she said. 'I may give it a miss, if you don't mind.'

He had been about to open his locker but he stopped and stared at her. 'Why?' he said quickly. 'Aren't you well?'

'No, I'm fine,' she said hastily. 'It's nothing like that...'

'Then what?' he persisted.

'It's nothing really—I just thought I may have an early night, that's all. It's been a long day,' she added.

She knew it sounded weak, an excuse, but how could she tell him—how could she begin to explain what she was really feeling? That because of the coolness, the politeness, which had grown between them she was finding it increasingly difficult to spend time with him when they were away from work—intimate time, which tonight would be because, with a disco at the barbeque, dancing would be inevitable.

Siobhan wasn't at all sure she could cope with Dave holding her close—the feel of his arms around her, his cheek against hers—knowing all the time that the relationship wasn't going anywhere and that eventually it would come to an end.

Maybe it would simply be better to end it now—go through the pain that would bring and then, hopefully, get her life back to what it had been before she had set eyes on Dave Morey.

'I want you to go,' he said quietly.

'I...'

'Please, Siobhan.'

She sighed, powerless to argue with him. 'I shall have to go home first and change.'

'I'll follow you,' said Dave, 'then we can go in my car. I would think the parking is limited, anyway.'

'Where is the barbeque?' Siobhan suddenly realised she hadn't any idea and would have probably assumed, if she'd been asked, that it would be held in the grounds of the Shalbrooke.

'It's on the beach,' Dave replied. 'Down at the cove.'

Dusk was already beginning to fall when they reached The Coach House, and all was in darkness. Chester barked once as Dave parked his car then was silent.

'Helen will be at the barbeque,' called Siobhan as she got out of her own car. 'I'll just go upstairs and change. I won't be long.'

She was true to her word, and very soon she had joined Dave and they were heading for the coast.

'You look lovely,' he said, taking his eyes briefly from the road and throwing her an appreciative glance.

Considering the short space of time she'd taken to get ready, the compliment was unexpected but pleasing. She wore black jeans and a black skinny rib top with a low scooped neckline. She'd tied back the wild mass of her red hair with a velvet ribbon, and at the last minute she'd grabbed a cotton sweater which she wore loosely around her shoulders.

Dave also wore jeans but his were traditional denim, which he wore with a red shirt which had the top buttons undone and the cuffs turned back to the elbow. Something about the sight of his arms, bronzed by the sun with a light covering of dark hair, made Siobhan's pulse race a little faster. Hastily she looked away.

The road to the cove was made even narrower than usual by the long line of cars parked down one side. They joined the end of the line and Dave switched off the engine and the lights.

'Looks like there's a good crowd down there,' he said, as they stepped out of the car. 'I dare say Pete will be glad to see me. I hope he's been able to cope and that it hasn't all been too much for him.'

He took her hand and together they made their way to the end of the road and the start of the long grassy slope.

The sound of Oasis filled the air, and long before they reached the beach they could see the glow of the bar-beque fires which had been set up in the shelter of the rocks. Fairy lights ran from the café to the clubhouse, adding a festive air to the occasion, and as they approached an appetising aroma of sausages, onions and burgers assailed their nostrils, tantalising their taste buds.

'There's Pete over there,' said Dave, as they walked over the soft, dry sand.

Siobhan looked up and saw that the disco had been set up against the rocks. 'He looks OK,' she said. 'Isn't that Sue helping him?'

'It is,' said Dave, with a chuckle. 'There was obviously no way either of them wanted Barry Weston taking over.'

The tide was out and couples danced on the wet sand against the magnificent backdrop of the Solent, with lighted vessels in its shipping lanes, and beyond that the myriad twinkling lights of the mainland.

Siobhan stopped for a moment simply to stand and stare. 'It's lovely,' she said. 'Quite lovely.'

'Glad you came?' asked Dave, squeezing her hand.

'Yes,' she replied, just loud enough for him to hear above the music. 'Yes, I believe I am.'

And quite suddenly she was. It didn't matter that this might not last. That the days of their relationship were probably numbered. She would deal with that when it happened. The only thing that really mattered was that, for the moment, the man she loved was at her side and the beat of the music was exciting, so exciting that she was afraid she was ready to throw caution to the winds.

CHAPTER TWELVE

'YOU'RE not going to believe this.' Dave grinned as he rejoined her, after speaking to Pete and Sue.

'Try me,' said Siobhan.

'Not only are those two managing perfectly well on their own—they don't even want any help, let alone letting me take over. They've told me to go away and have fun.'

'So, is that what you intend doing?' She smiled up at him.

'Just try stopping me. Come on, let's get some food before it's all gone. I'm starving and you must be the same.' Taking her hand and not waiting for an answer, he led her across the beach to the barbeques. Georgina Merrick was helping to dispense hot dogs and burgers. She smiled a greeting when she saw Dave and Siobhan.

'Hi, you two,' she said. 'What would you like?'

As she filled paper plates for them both and passed them cans of shandy, Siobhan looked round at the throng of people. 'Is Helen here, Georgina?' she said.

'No, I don't think so, not yet,' Georgina replied. 'I thought she would have been by now. She went to see her father after work.'

'Oh, I see,' said Siobhan. 'Well, let's hope she gets here soon, otherwise the food will have all gone.'

They carried their food to one of the clusters of large rocks where they sat on the soft sand, listening to the music and watching the dancers and the sea, dark and satiny tonight with no windsurfers planing its surface like so many dragonflies.

Greg Freeman was among the dancers, with his red-haired receptionist. He appeared to be having a good time until he looked up and, catching sight of Siobhan, seemed covered in sudden embarrassment. Josh Meecher was also there with his wife, Emma, but there was no sign of Barry Weston.

'Probably sulking,' said Dave, when Siobhan commented on the fact.

'Maybe dancing just isn't his scene,' she replied, licking her fingers as she finished her food.

'No, probably not, but it sure as hell is mine.' Dave got to his feet and, reaching down, took her hands to pull her up beside him. 'Come on, there's nothing like a bit of Eric Clapton to get me going.' He led her down onto the vast patch of wet sand, where he drew her into his arms.

Helplessly she leaned against him, content for the moment to rest her head on his shoulder and for them both to give themselves up to the sensual beat of the music. They stayed like that, entwined in each other's arms, for a very long time as one music track followed another. Then, as the pace quickened, they drew apart slightly and Dave looked over her shoulder.

'Well,' he said, 'that's a relief.'

'What is?' Siobhan looked up into his eyes.

'Zoe Grainger dancing with her husband, Mal.'

'You mean they're back together again?' Siobhan's eyes widened.

'It looks like it—they're all over each other.'

'Has she seen us?' asked Siobhan tentatively.

'Yes,' Dave replied. 'She spotted us soon after we

arrived. I nodded at her, but she ignored me and looked the other way.'

'I bet you were upset.'

'Devastated.' He chuckled and drew her close again. 'I must admit I hadn't realised then that she was with Mal.'

'And how do you feel about that?'

'I hope it lasts this time,' he replied. 'After all, they are married, and in my book marriage is for keeps.'

'Is that why you've never married?'

'Probably.'

'Because the commitment is too great?' she whispered.

'No.' He held her even closer, so close that she could feel his heart beating. 'Because I hadn't found anyone I would want to spend the rest of my life with.'

His lips found hers in the darkness, and as she gave herself up to the thrill of his kiss a shaft of raw desire spread through her veins like wildfire and her longing for him almost overwhelmed her.

'You know something, Siobhan?' he whispered, his voice husky. 'I'm not sure I can stand much more of this. I love you and I want you so very much.'

They left the barbeque soon after that, walking out of the cove and back to the car, their arms entwined.

On the drive back to The Coach House all the old agonies returned. She knew she loved him, wanted him, just as much as he wanted her. Should she just give in—forget the promise she had made to herself and simply live for the moment?

If she didn't she might never know what it would be like to be loved by him and maybe live to regret that fact for the rest of her life. He'd just said he couldn't stand the situation for much longer which, no doubt, meant he was on the point of ending the relationship.

She stared through the windscreen at the road ahead with unseeing eyes.

If he did that—told her he didn't want to see her again—she didn't think she would be able to bear it. It was up to her now. It seemed only she had the power to change things.

They turned into the drive of The Coach House, and as Dave brought his car to a halt Siobhan was vaguely aware that there were lights on in the house and that there were three cars in the drive. If she hadn't been so preoccupied with her own dilemma she might have thought that odd and wondered why Helen hadn't gone to the barbeque. As it was, she hardly noticed, turning instead to Dave as he switched off the engine.

'Dave,' she began, 'I've been thinking...' She got no further because he silenced her with a kiss.

It started as a gentle kiss, a tender kiss, but it rapidly changed as the ready passion flared again between them until, with a desperate groan, Dave pulled away from her.

'Siobhan, stop it,' he protested. 'You've completely bewitched me, and if you carry on like this I can't be held responsible for my actions...'

'That's what I was about to say...' she began, but still he wouldn't let her finish.

'I shall take you up to that flat, tear all your clothes off and make passionate love to you. And then...'

'Yes...?'

'Then I shall do it all over again.'

'Oh,' she said. 'Oh, yes.'

'But I'm not going to do that.' Visibly he struggled for control.

'You're not?' She tried to keep the disappointment out of her voice but feared she'd failed miserably.

'No,' he said firmly. 'And do you want to know why I'm not going to do that?'

She nodded, her eyes widening as she wondered what he was going to say.

'Because you've totally enchanted me, Siobhan, and part of that enchantment is because you are so different from any other girl I have ever known.' His voice caught in his throat. 'I couldn't understand you at first and I'm not sure I do now, but somehow that just adds to your mystery. I love you and I want you, but...' he held his fingers to her lips as she made to speak again '...not now. Like you, I'm prepared to wait. It'll probably kill me, but our wedding night will be all the better for the waiting.'

She stared at him in shocked silence, totally lost for words.

He must have misunderstood her silence because he caught her hand, and in the half-light, anxiously scanning her features, he said, 'I know we haven't known each other for very long, but I don't need any longer. I know you're the girl for me—the girl I have been waiting for all my life. Siobhan, you will marry me, won't you?'

'Oh, yes,' she whispered, her reply as inevitable as the tide as it swept the shore. 'Of course I will.'

He drew her into his arms again, and his mouth covered hers in a long kiss. When at last they drew reluctantly apart he gave a soft chuckle.

'What is it?' she asked.

'I was just wondering...' he glanced over his shoulder towards the house '...what Helen will say.'

'Heavens,' said Siobhan. 'I can't imagine.'

'Maybe we should go and tell her now. Maybe it will soften the blow if she thinks she's the first to know.'

'Yes, maybe,' replied Siobhan dubiously.

'On the other hand,' said Dave as they got out of the car, 'it looks like she may have company. Isn't that Richard Fleetwood's car?'

Siobhan nodded, 'Yes, it is. I'm not sure about the other one, though.'

'That looks like Kate Chapman's,' said Dave, 'although I can't be certain.'

'I know Kate is a friend of Helen's,' said Siobhan. 'What I don't understand is why none of them were at the barbeque. I don't suppose it would exactly be Richard Fleetwood's scene, but I thought Helen would have roped them all in, especially as it was for charity. And Helen herself should certainly have been there—'

'Someone's coming out now,' said Dave suddenly, as the front door opened.

Kate Chapman appeared in the porch. She peered into the darkness, her face clearing when she caught sight of them.

'Oh, Dave, it's you,' she said, 'and Siobhan. I'm so glad you're back. I have to go now and Richard is on call.'

'What is it?' asked Siobhan, staring at Kate. Even before the doctor answered some sixth sense warned her what she was about to hear.

'Harry Turner died this evening,' she said. 'Helen is very upset.'

'I'll go to her,' said Siobhan. As Kate got into her car Siobhan was aware of Dave by her side, his hand comfortingly under her elbow, and fleetingly it occurred to her that from now this was how it would always be.

After Richard Fleetwood left it was Dave who took

control, Dave who brewed countless cups of tea and Dave who offered comfort and support to the two cousins in their shared grief.

'He's at peace now, Helen,' he said. 'No more pain, no more frustration, no more loss of dignity.'

'I know.' Helen stared into the depths of her almost empty mug. 'I know, Dave, and for that I'm thankful. I am, I really am.

'It's just that…' She hesitated, and they both listened waiting for her to continue. 'I thought I would know when it was imminent—I am a nurse, for heaven's sake—but I didn't. When I saw him yesterday he was no different from what he has been for weeks so, you see, there wasn't any extra warning. Then early this evening I got a phone call from the ward sister to say he was deteriorating. Even then I didn't fully grasp the implications. I thought any deterioration would be slow—just like it's been all along.

'And do you know?' Helplessly, her eyes swimming with tears, she looked up at Dave and then at Siobhan, who sat beside her on the sofa in her sitting room. 'Even then, with all my training, I didn't know. I thought he would pull through again.'

'I don't think training comes into it when it's someone of your own,' said Dave quietly. 'I reckon that part of your brain becomes frozen and all you can do is pray that everything will be all right.'

Siobhan looked up at him for a long moment as Helen began speaking again.

'I guess,' she said slowly, 'praying was probably all I was capable of.'

Ever since they had arrived Chester had been sitting beside his mistress, his head resting on her knee as he gazed dolefully into her face. Absent-mindedly she now began to stroke the dog's silky ears. 'You'll miss him too, won't you, old boy?' she said.

'You were there in time?' asked Siobhan suddenly, anxiously.

'Oh, yes,' said Helen. 'I was in time. Not that he knew I was there, of course. He was unconscious by the time I got there, but even if he hadn't been I doubt he would have known who I was... We were very close, you know.' She looked up at Dave as she spoke. 'Especially since Mum died.'

'Yes,' he said gently. 'That was obvious to everyone, Helen.'

'Was it?' She looked faintly surprised as, leaning forward again, she said, 'I shall miss him terribly.'

Helplessly they watched as her tears fell onto Chester's head and disappeared into the dog's rich copper coat.

They didn't tell Helen their news that night, nor in the days that followed immediately preceding Harry Turner's funeral, but there came a point when Siobhan realised they could delay no longer.

'My family will come over for the funeral,' she told Dave late one evening as they sat in his car on the cliff-top and watched the sun set. 'Afterwards, I shall need to tell them about us.'

'In that case,' said Dave, 'I think Helen should know before they arrive.' He hesitated. 'Would you like me to tell her?'

Siobhan shook her head. 'No,' she said, 'I think I should be the one to do it.'

'I know she doesn't approve of me,' said Dave slowly after a moment, 'and I can't honestly say I blame her, not with my track record.'

'Her approval shouldn't matter,' said Siobhan. 'After all, it isn't as if I'm under age or anything, but…'

'It does matter, doesn't it?' Stretching out his hand he gently ran the back of his fingers down her cheek.

'Yes,' she admitted at last with a little sigh, 'in a funny sort of way it does. I'm very fond of Helen and I know my mother is as well. She sets great store by what Helen says.'

'So she's bound to be influenced by Helen's opinion of the man her only daughter wants to marry.'

'Yes, I guess that's about it.'

They fell silent again and Dave turned to look at her. 'Will your brothers be coming over as well?' he asked.

'Probably.'

Sharply he drew in his breath. 'In that case,' he said, 'I think it might be best if I made my self scarce for a few days—you know, get out of town before they run me out.'

'Oh, Dave, no.' Laughingly she protested. 'I want you to meet them all, and when they know how much I love you and that you are the man I'm going to marry they will want to meet you—and at least this way you get to meet them all before the wedding day, even if the circumstances are sad.'

She was silent for a moment, before, with a tentative glance in his direction, she went on. 'Speaking of the wedding, Dave, my parents will want me to have a full church wedding at home in Ireland…'

'And is that what you want?' he asked quietly, seriously.

'Yes, Dave,' she said, 'it is. It is what I have always wanted.'

'I thought it might be,' he said, adding simply, 'In that case, that's what it'll be.'

'I didn't think you'd agree,' she said.

'Why not?' He grinned. 'I'm not such a heathen as all that, you know.'

'I didn't ever think you were,' she said happily, leaning forward for his kiss. 'Not for one moment.'

'You're going to marry him, aren't you?'

It was the following day. Siobhan and Helen were taking an early morning walk in the woods behind The Coach House, Chester padding silently between them, when quite suddenly Helen posed the question that Siobhan had been wondering how she could raise. She threw her cousin a startled glance, but was surprised to find she appeared neither shocked nor even particularly surprised.

'Yes,' she admitted, 'yes, I am. But how did you know?'

'It's been written all over your faces for the past few days.'

'Oh, dear, we didn't realise it was that obvious. I'm sorry, Helen,' she said in dismay, 'we didn't mean it to be, not with what has happened.'

'Life has to go on, Siobhan. My father would have been the first to say that.'

'Yes...I know...' Siobhan paused and looked curiously at Helen. 'You don't sound as if you're too bothered about the fact that I'm to marry Dave. I thought you'd be annoyed. In fact, I wasn't looking forward to telling you.' She hesitated. 'Or is it that you've just become resigned to something you can't change?' she added.

'I'm not sure how I feel, exactly,' said Helen.

They walked on in silence for a while, their feet making no noise on the soft earth of the woodland path, the only sound that of a blackbird's song as he accompanied them on their walk, flitting alongside them from branch to branch.

'At first, you know,' Helen went on at last, 'I was horrified at the thought of you becoming involved with Dave Morey.'

Siobhan smiled. 'I know,' she said. 'In fact, so much so that I think it was your warnings that got me interested in the first place. I was intrigued with this man who had apparently broken so many hearts.'

Helen gave a rueful sigh. 'In a way, I suppose I was responsible, yet again, for playing the matchmaker—even if it was inadvertently.'

'Yes, I guess you could say that.' Siobhan chuckled. Growing serious again, she said, 'On the other hand, I know you only had my best interests at heart and all your warnings were given with the best of intentions...'

'But, quite obviously, to no avail...' said Helen drily.

'I love him, Helen,' said Siobhan. 'And he loves me. So much so that he wants to marry me.'

'In the past Dave Morey has never made any bones about the fact that he isn't the marrying kind,' said Helen.

'I know. He told me that at first, but he says that was before...before he met me... He says it's all changed now...he's changed.' Siobhan stopped suddenly and threw up her hands. 'Oh, I know you probably think that sounds ridiculous...that I'm being hopelessly naïve...' She threw Helen a sharp glance, fully expecting to see a sceptical look on her face. Instead, to her surprise she found a smile, a gentle, understanding smile.

'No,' said Helen, 'as it happens, I don't think it's ridiculous. I also think he may have changed—that meeting a girl he truly loves has given him a different perspective on love, on sex and on marriage.

'And, I have to admit,' she went on when Siobhan remained silent, 'I've seen a different side to him lately. Take the other night, for example...after Dad died. He was so kind. I would never have believed him capable of such depths of compassion.'

'Oh, Helen, he is,' Siobhan cried. 'And when you really get to know him you'll see even more. And it is all going to work out for us, I just know it is.'

'Yes,' said Helen, 'I believe it will.' She paused and as Chester gave a short sharp bark, adding his seal of approval, she added fiercely, 'And if it doesn't, if he breaks your heart, he has me to answer to—just as I told him when you first started going out with him.'

Siobhan stared at her. 'Helen,' she said, 'you didn't!'

'Didn't I?' said Helen darkly. 'You just ask him.'

Bright early morning sunlight shimmered on the surface of the water while the waves lapped gently over the board and Siobhan's feet. A deceptively playful breeze carried her in a great arc as she planed the waves. Briefly she glanced at the only other figure in sight and he raised one arm pointing to indicate what path they would follow.

It had been Dave's idea that morning to go to the beaches in the south-west of the Island—wide beaches off the old military road where huge waves rolled timelessly beneath sandstone cliffs, scene of many shipwrecks in the past.

They had gone alone, needing time together after the recent trauma of Harry Turner's death, his funeral and the inevitable gathering of the Turners and the O'Maras. Her family had returned to Ireland now to make prepa-

'Oh, at least,' he said solemnly. Gently he drew her into his arms while the water from their wetsuits continued to form a puddle around them, which in turn seeped quietly away into the sand.

'You know something, Siobhan O'Mara?' he said at last. 'I told you once that you'd bewitched me with your Irish charm, didn't I?'

'Yes, Mr Morey,' she replied. 'I do believe you did.'

'Well,' he went on, taking her face between both his hands and lifting it to his own, 'I still believe that because it can be the only explanation for what has happened to me in the last few weeks. To make me feel the way I do every time I look into those lovely eyes of yours…but, quite apart from all that, to know that, unbelievably, the best is still to come.'

'Oh, yes,' said Siobhan, with a little sigh of pure contentment. 'The best most certainly is still to come.'

With a delicious thrill of anticipation she parted her lips, and as she waited for his kiss the foaming breakers continued to roll in behind them onto the beach and the sunlight still danced on the vast blue expanse of the sea.

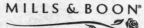

MILLS & BOON®

Sizzle

Soak up the sun with the
perfect summer read

Four sizzling short stories in one volume—
perfect for lazing on the beach or in the garden.

A combination of young, fresh, talented authors
led by Jennifer Crusie—one of our most
popular Temptation® writers.

*Look out for Sizzle in August 1998 by
Jennifer Crusie, Carrie Alexander,
Ellen Rogers and Annie Sims*

RONA JAFFE

Five Women

Once a week, five women meet over dinner and
drinks at the Yellowbird, their favourite
Manhattan bar. To the shared table they bring
their troubled pasts; their hidden secrets.
And through their friendship, each will find
a courageous new beginning.

Five Women is an *"insightful look at female
relationships."*

—Publishers Weekly

1-55166-424-0
**AVAILABLE IN PAPERBACK
FROM AUGUST, 1998**

DEBBIE MACOMBER

Married in Montana

Needing a safe place for her sons to grow up, Molly
Cogan decided it was time to return home.
Home to Sweetgrass Montana.
Home to her grandfather's ranch.

*"Debbie Macomber's name on a book is a guarantee
of delightful, warm-hearted romance."*

—Jayne Ann Krentz

1-55166-400-3
**AVAILABLE IN PAPERBACK
FROM AUGUST, 1998**

4 FREE

books and a surprise gift!

We would like to take this opportunity to thank you for reading this Mills & Boon® book by offering you the chance to take FOUR more specially selected titles from the Medical Romance™ series absolutely FREE! We're also making this offer to introduce you to the benefits of the Reader Service™—

★ FREE home delivery
★ FREE gifts and competitions
★ FREE monthly newsletter
★ Books available before they're in the shops
★ Exclusive Reader Service discounts

Accepting these FREE books and gift places you under no obligation to buy, you may cancel at any time, even after receiving your free shipment. Simply complete your details below and return the entire page to the address below. *You don't even need a stamp!*

YES! Please send me 4 free Medical Romance books and a surprise gift. I understand that unless you hear from me, I will receive 4 superb new titles every month for just £2.30 each, postage and packing free. I am under no obligation to purchase any books and may cancel my subscription at any time. The free books and gift will be mine to keep in any case.

M8YE

Ms/Mrs/Miss/Mr.............................Initials ....
BLOCK CAPITALS PLEASE

Surname ....

Address ....

....

....Postcode...........................

Send this whole page to:
THE READER SERVICE, FREEPOST, CROYDON, CR9 3WZ
(Eire readers please send coupon to: P.O. BOX 4546, DUBLIN 24.)